QUANTUM DEADLINE

THE LUMAVILLE LABYRINTH
PART ONE

DAEDALUS HOWELL

FMRL
FUTURE MEDIA RESEARCH LAB

By the Same Author

The Late Projectionist
I Heart Sonoma: How to Live & Drink in Wine Country

QUANTUM DEADLINE

THE LUMAVILLE LABYRINTH
PART ONE

DAEDALUS HOWELL

FMRL
FUTURE MEDIA RESEARCH LAB

Quantum Deadline

FMRL | P.O. Box 5427 | Berkeley CA 94705

fmrl.com

ISBN-10:0-9671001-7-8
ISBN-13:978-0-9671001-7-3
Library of Congress Control Number 2015908076

Designed by Kit Fergus
Labyrinth logo designed by Shauna Haider.

This is a work of fiction. Names, characters, businesses, places, events and incidents are either the products of the author's imagination or used in a fictitious manner. Any resemblance to actual persons, living or dead, or actual events is purely coincidental.

The author gratefully acknowledges the contributions of Dennis Ferguson, Irène Hodes, AJ Petersen, Lisa Summers, Dmitra Smith, Stacey Tuel, Jonah Raskin and W.B. Yeats.

Visit DaedalusHowell.com.

QUANTUM DEADLINE

THE LUMAVILLE LABYRINTH
PART ONE

DAEDALUS HOWELL

Contents

On Background— 11

The Fit— 14

The Editrix— 19

Fauxbituary— 24

Call Me— 26

Happy Birthday, Mr. McCormack— 36

Dewey Wins— 42

Inverting Pyramids— 58

Dr(ink)— 66

Welcoming Committee— 72

The Knights of Skeldaria— 84

We Can Be Heroes— 90

Needle in a Haymaker— 101

Heave Ho— 109

Big Box— 114

FMRL— 121
The Penultimate Integer— 133
Intermission— 145
Murderer's Thumb— 161
The Short Goodbye— 169
Smoke— 181
To Catch a Train— 185
Well Hung— 194
Storage— 203
Come up to the Lab— 213
Novus Alarum— 218
In the Key of Block— 230
On Deadline— 238
Next— 243

For C.F.

For the world's more full of weeping than you can understand.

Based on a true story. Somewhere.

1.

On Background

Early in my career, I was a green reporter who wrote purple prose that read like yellow journalism. But they printed the paper in black and white so no one ever noticed.

Now, I was just a hack, one who needed a story and needed it bad. The problem, as always, is that I'm not the type to make my own breaks. I'm not inclined to write a bogus memoir, say, or parade as a pillhead or claim to be the last, lone believer in my generation. I'm also not opportunistic enough to know a good thing when I've got it, so whatever it is, it won't make it into print – or pixels – let alone a bestseller list. Even if it did, the editors wouldn't believe it. Such is the hazard of being in the *truth* business, not the *fact* business.

Forgive me. I buried the lede...

You see, back in J-School, in the 90s, my future colleagues and I knew nothing of the then-nascent Internet and the havoc it would wreak on our prospective industry. Now, there's an entire generation that has never read a printed newspaper. And they're the ones *running* the papers. Or what's left of them.

This is how I found myself on the lifestyle beat for a

startup that required endless filing of snark and crap that met certain considerations of "keyword density" and adhered to the house style of punchy prose that was neither punchy nor prose by any definition of contemporary letters. IMHO. For the past five years, the work had been winnowed, watered and weighed down in equal measure. For the past five years, I've been in psychic exile. For the past five years, I've been leaning on a pseudonym to make the rent because...

I also buried an intern.

This is the truth. When you fail to talk your newsroom intern out of jumping off the Golden Gate Bridge, prepare yourself for the following: Your intern will be dead, your career will be over and your newspaper will fold. And not into a paper hat.

That's really how I became a small town newspaperman without a town or a newspaper. I'm sure some even questioned whether I had the moral ground to call myself a man.

With some modest triangulating on Google, it could be known that I was the writer who whose words – my stock and trade – had utterly failed to talk a young man out of taking two steps back onto the bridge's pedestrian walkway and into the rest of his young life.

"Is it going to get better, the newspaper, life, all of this?" he spat against the wind as it whipped his hair against his 21-year-old forehead.

"No. It's only going to get worse."

"Then why do we do it?" he asked.

I didn't have an answer. Or, I did, but it wasn't the right answer. He shifted his grip and the sweat from his palms darkened the rust-hue of the girder. I improvised.

"Deadlines...?"

This much is certain: It was not the answer he was seeking.

He let go and in one glib moment, with no foresight and no hindsight of which to speak, changed both of our lives forever.

There's more, but we'll get to that. What's germane is from that moment hence I'd been searching for a story – a new story that would make my past and failures a footnote to the shiny future I'd lost, that my intern lost, that everyone lost. Really, my new story needed to be an old story: a redemption tale, as they say in Hollywood; one with enough truth and triumph to clear my byline so that, among other advantages, I might use it again.

I found the story. Or, I could get cute and say the story found me. Apparently, that's an antimetabole. Some day I might look it up to prove it. In the meantime (not to fracture the fourth wall into constituent fractals of meaning) the story begins, as these things do, in a mirror.

2.
The Fit

There's a kind of guy who can wear a cheap suit well and I like to pretend I'm him. Frankly, I had no choice, especially after I burned a cigarette hole through my last good blazer and I have an image to maintain. I am among the last of a dying breed of lifestyle reporters, feature writers who, as one neckbearded editor put it, "grok the grub and grog," which always sounded to me like the sounds of someone being strangled. But it's a living. Or was. Hence, my pitstop at Gemelli Bros.

The discount suitery was owned by a pair of oily identical twins squeezed into double-breasted suits who called themselves Tweedle Deep and Tweedle Dump in their local television ads. Tweedle Deep, I think, was marking up my new coat with chalk when it happened.

"You like a little room in the chestal area?" he asked, tugging at the coat's hem. I stood still in the three way mirror like a human mannequin if they made them in my size, 44 long, wide in the shoulders, taller than most, which made the gut passable if I never exhaled.

"I've gotta fit a reporter's notebook in my left breast pocket," I said. "And a pen."

The man grunted and swiftly drew an X over my heart.

"I never met a newspaperman before," he said. He was being facetious, as if "newspaperman" was what a paperboy grew up to be.

The phone rang and the man trundled off through the maze of suits crowded on their racks like delicatessen salamis.

In the mirror, I was surprised at how relatively good I looked despite the night before. I outstretched my arms and the black coat opened crisply like an umbrella. I surmised from the inexpensive blend of polymers that the coat was waterproof.

The fat clothier brayed into the phone. His tone was heated. I entertained myself by maneuvering the hinged mirrors, flanking the one in the middle so that my reflection went from triplicate to infinite. This is how I used to kill time when my mother dragged me to department stores when I was a kid. For that matter, it's how I kept from losing my mind when my ex took me on forced marches through the junior's department whose trendy tops and shrinking bottoms she could still pull off in her thirties.

I began to entomb myself in the mirrors, creating hundreds of images of myself – rumpled, debauched but serviceably handsome to a certain type of woman. One whose standards have been systematically lowered by being born Gen X and coming of age under the sign of Slack.

An intruder entered my chamber of narcissism. A small quizzical face beamed back at me through the corner of the left mirror. It was a boy of about eleven with dark hair and a tailored blue suit with a badge on the pocket.

He shook his head. I straightened, reflexively, as if he'd caught me picking my nose. I turned from my personal Escher print and spied him standing outside the store window staring at me like I was a ghost or he was a ghost or... I couldn't take it.

15

I flipped him off.

I expected the kid to do the same back at me. Instead he shouted "Down!" At least that's what it looked like he said. I couldn't hear him through the window. Besides, it sounded like a walnut had just been cracked upside my head. The mirror behind me shattered.

"You fuggin' asshole!" boomed through the coat shop, punctuated with another shot. This one sounded like a fist deep in a down pillow.

I was on the floor, belly down, atop saber-length shards of broken mirror. My knees had buckled autonomically. Was I shot? I rolled behind a rack and patted myself down. Not even a scratch from the glass. I looked up and saw my tailor clutching his gut.

"She's my wife!" the shooter said. His tone was one of defeat.

Tweedle Dump kept the gun trained on his twin brother. Two thoughts crossed my mind simultaneously. A) They should have incorporated some of this sibling rivalry shit into their TV commercials and B) Where was the kid? I belly-crawled to the coat rack as another shot rang through the shop. Tweedle Deep wheezed, "Fuck you too." I peeked through the size 34 slacks. He had a small pistol weighing in his pudgy hand. He dropped to his knees as his porcine twin glowered back, his white shirt now a rising tide of blood and bile.

"That's not going to come out," Tweedle Dump observed before also falling to his knees, his bulk jiggling like a massive water balloon. After a beat, both Gemelli twins collapsed onto the beige berber carpet in a puddle of oily, brown blood.

A store clerk with pasted-down hair wandered into the front door and calmly observed dead orcas draining on the floor. He called 911, but not before calling his girlfriend to tell her to stay in bed, because he was taking the day off. He looked at me and shook his head. "It was going to happen sooner or later. Lucky you didn't get hit. Them brothers was as blind as shit."

"I'm fine," I said as I unfolded back onto my feet. "There was a kid in the window, you see him?"

"I didn't see a kid. If he was here, he was gone when I got here. If he's a neighborhood kid this ain't nothing he hasn't seen before. Had the good sense to run," he said matter-of-factly. "Probably home doing instant replays on his video game machine."

* * *

When the police arrived, they cordoned off the crime scene with yellow tape until it looked like a cat's cradle. They took pictures and proceeded to fill paper cups with coffee from a large press pot.

"That press pot is the most important part of our forensics kit," explained Detective Shane. She was black, rounder than perhaps she cared to be and appeared young for her rank, which is to say, younger than me. "You put shit in it?"

I looked at her blankly and she handed me a cup of black coffee.

"So, you say there was a kid? Did he witness the shooting too?"

"I'm not sure. It all..."

"Happened so fast. I know. Bullets are like that. Well, we put a car out looking for him and no one's turned up. Should be in school anyway," she said.

I nodded and sipped the coffee. The detective watched me sip.

"It's good, isn't it?" she said proudly. "Our department has the best coffee in the East Bay.

"What's your secret?"

"We give a fuck. That's all. You just gotta give a fuck." She folded up her notebook. "Listen, I've got your statement. You're not a suspect, the security cameras confirm that. I might need you to come down to the station later for more details, especially if the kid turns up, but otherwise, you're free to go."

"Does it matter that I'm a member of the media?" I asked for no good reason. Maybe I wanted to seem in the game – that I wasn't just a civilian. Shane gave me a once-over.

"In that jacket?" she quipped, then caught herself reflected in my eyes. "It's really that bad for you guys, isn't it?"

I nodded, "Just me." But I knew my luck was beginning to turn and that kid who should've been in school was part of it.

3.
The Editrix

The home office of the Lumaville blog was neither an office nor a home to anyone who'd ever paid rent. It was a large, wide-open, glorified squat with exposed brick and ducting, but not in the chi-chi way that might attract the gentrifying forces of arts and commerce. It was a demolition project that was canceled midstream by some historical society or other and divvied up into a warren of offices for nonprofits. Throughout the space, the young leaders of tomorrow clicked and swiped on devices at scattered desks. Adriane, my editor, sat at her desk, her eyes downcast, wriggling her nose. Could she smell me? She flashed her palm at me, signalling me to halt whatever it was I was about to do, which was what I always did: waited for Adriane to acknowledge my existence.

Since the collapse of my career as a newspaperman occurred at about the same time the industry as a whole was in a tailspin, it was easy to camouflage my failure. I was going from bylines to breadlines like the rest of print media. Ours was an industry of dinosaurs, though not all dinosaurs went extinct. Some evolved into birds, some even tweeted.

Adriane was all of 24 years old. Her expensive school

back east offered a specialty in online journalism, PR and social media marketing – as if they were all one enterprise. Some jack-hole gave these kids a few million dollars to beta test a "hyperlocal online news portal" that proffered coverage "by you and for you."

When I was her age, we referred to anything related to the then-nascent Internet as "cyber," which now sounds as antiquated as applying "horseless" to anything that no longer needed a horse. Though it had only been a few months since its launch, the "hyperlocal online new portal" was already beginning to seem like it was lacking in the equine department.

"I'm editing your latest piece," she said as her eyes became two glassy moons. Was that moisture, I thought? Had I actually moved this chick, who was otherwise an Easter Island moai? She wiped her eyes on the sleeve of her hoodie.

"Your piece made my eyes water," she sighed. "It's really, really long. I had to take half an Adderall to finish it. We need punchy, quick, dirty and click, we're outta there. I mean, is this even true?"

I couldn't remember for the life of me what piece-of-shit story of mine she might have read. It was clear from the onset of our working together that she thought I was not contemporary enough and that I should get back in my cyber-horseless carriage and fuck off to wherever it was from whence I came. Which would be the 90s.

Despite my 15 years as an itinerant newspaperman for alternative newsweeklies (for which I won no fewer than two awards, one national at that), it seemed I had gotten somehow out of joint with the world. I used to love freelancing. In fact, when I was at the paper, I'd lament how I missed the freedom of freelancing, which I'd come to believe was like some sort of careerist Nirvana the way some married people remember being single. Clearly, there was something I just didn't get. An ingredient was missing, there was something in my prime directive that wasn't syncing with that of my latest editorial dalliance. My provenance as a print journalist had become a liability. Mere mention of newspapers brings visions of useless pica poles and "Blue Streak" pens to the minds of digital natives who have "an app for that."

This was my latest attempt to string, post-implosion of the Lumaville Daily Echo and my career along with it. This time, there was a palpable rift between me and everything I thought was happening in the lifestyle game. I'd been up on every shift no matter how minor or seismic. Yet, this particular tour of duty made it clear: I was out of touch.

No matter what new app, social-something or whatever, I no longer could keep up. As Detective Shane would say, I didn't "give a fuck." It was my own fault, or at least the fault of my generation. We pushed hard, and rightly so, against malingering boomers with our technology and other accelerants only to have their younger spawn, the Millennials, come back to avenge them. The kids were barely done sucking the thumbs they use to text each other and now I was under one.

"What's with the 'X' on your jacket?" Adriane asked. I had no idea what she was talking about. She gestured to her chest. It took an awkward moment of squinting at her perky young boobs before I finally looked at my own chest. Indeed, there was an X on my pocket drawn by the dead clothier. It was then that I realized I had effectively stolen the jacket, in front of a cop no less. Good for me. There was also the added bonus of a having a story.

"I witnessed a shootout between a pair of twin tailors in the garment district."

Adriane seemed uncharacteristically intrigued.

"Were they Siamese twins?" she asked.

"No, just a couple of fat guys."

"How fat? Sideshow fat?"

"Just normal fat. '*Murican* fat."

"I only like to run true crime if it's cannibals or Darwin Award winners," she said. Her eyes narrowed on me until they looked like a pair of Inuit snow goggles.

"You know what you *could* do," she said. "You could get me that interview with Cameron Block you promised. You know, the one that got you the job. How 'bout that?"

Worse than failing at life so epically is failing in front of your successful friends. I'd known Cameron Block since college – or more specifically – the years we spent together in college before he left to win fame and fortune in the dot-com boom-and-bust, and I dropped out to take a job at the Lumaville Daily Echo.

Somehow we were both friends and rivals. And the galling part was he didn't seem aware of either. This made me hate him that crucial bit more than I hated myself when I was in his company. And though I hadn't spoken to him in years, I name-dropped him every time I needed to impress an editor. Or felt the need to kill a little part of my soul.

Adriane didn't wait for an answer. Instead, she scrolled through her phone for keywords – what people were actually searching for online – so we could capture their traffic from search engines. From that she'd create a list of keyword-dense headlines and assign the "listicles" accordingly.

5 Ways to Lose Weight by Smoking

How to Earn $10k by Reading ebooks about Free ebooks in 3 Easy Steps

Adriane's phone dinged. She glanced at the message.

"It's a release from the cops. Not your fatty fratricide. 'Professor Ashe Still Missing.' Duh, because she's dead," Adriane sarcastically observed, more to herself than me.

"And boring." Another ding. "New surveillance cameras on the SMART train. And they got a mural."

"I can cover both with a 'watching paint dry' angle," I quipped.

Adriane thumbed something into her phone and then shook her head. "Yeah, no. Not enough search juice. Like I already knew."

She tossed the phone on her desk, then brightened when a printed release caught her eye. "How about the Centenarian birthday?"

"What, the guy's half horse?" I asked.

"He's turning 100," she all but spat. "That's worth a few hundred words on the 'milestones' category page. We had an ad buy there. Write it quickly."

My how the wall between editorial and advertising had crumbled, I thought. But "I'm not here to impress sponsors" is what I said.

"I mean, write it before the guy dies."

4.

Fauxbituary

I strolled into my first newsroom in the late 90s and was appalled to see that the layout team was using hand waxers and lightboxes. The newsroom was like a living history museum, with hacks wearing fedoras amongst the clickety-clack of typewriters. The desktop publishing revolution was nearly a decade old at that point and yet here was a "real" newspaper cutting and pasting like kindergartners. And now I was working with kindergartners.

All the desks were taken. The bean bags too. At Lumaville. com, we didn't have assigned working spaces. Instead, we had "company culture."

I went to a window so I could see the rooftop next to ours, a couple of stories below. There was a Chinese restaurant that ran a stove pipe from the grill hood to just below my nostrils. Consequently, that part of the building reeked of kitchen grease and chicken chow mein.

Since I billed hourly, I'd wait until I was at my desk to check my email. I waded through the usual spam about male enhancement and invitations from the prince of Nigeria to front him some cash.

Finally, a subject line floated up like a dead goldfish. It read, "Remembering Daedalus Howell." Finally, a fan letter. I considered deleting it. It was the first such email I'd received in recent weeks. I decided to read it to see if my condition had improved since the last two obituaries I had received. I read the first line.

Writer, raconteur and inveterate bore Daedalus Howell met an untimely end last night. The professional snark known mostly (if it all) for his saucy invectives published in alternative news weeklies of the sort used to blot spilled coffee on cafe counters, hastened his expiration by his own hand, thereby encircling his sex life and death in a perfect ring of shame. Howell is survived by the rats in the walls of his garret and the mountain debt of both the financial and karmic varieties. In death, he joins a career he killed five years prior. A memorial will be conducted at the G Street dock, where a garbage can will be lit in his honor. Donations can be sent to Lumaville Refuse Disposal, which now manages Howell's literary estate.

I dragged and dropped the email into the "Fauxbituary" file on my machine. I had received enough of these pithy missives to keep them all in the same batch since they far-and-away exceeded the usual complaints, diatribes and death wishes with their mirth and style. It was probably a former colleague who mistook it, as I did at first, for humor. Lots of things are funny at first – like sex, or making a quiche, and even an obituary with your own name on it. After a while, however, the obits became worrisome. Especially since they always arrived in my inbox marked "No Sender, No Subject." Obviously my obit-writer was some kind of hacker or time traveler. Or both.

5.
Call Me

My mobile rang. Detective Shane was on the line, laughing about something before she realized I had answered.

"Hey, Media Man – how's the jacket?"

"Busted," I thought.

"I'll return it. Should've gone double-vented anyway," I said and I meant it.

"Your tailor got double-vented and it didn't do him a lick of good," she said. "That's cop humor."

"How is he?"

"Still dead. So, I need you to come down to the station. We found the kid."

"So he's real then?" I said.

"Oh, yeah, he's real, but maybe *not for real*. He's a whole case unto himself," she said. "I need you to ID him so I can corroborate his story."

"He's got a story?" I asked. How is it everyone has a story except me?

"Well, he's got something," she said.

* * *

The Lumaville Police Department is located on the north end of the Boulevard on a sunny part of the street across from a diner doing its best to outshine the trappings of its former chain eatery architecture. Felons – murderers, rapists and exploiters of innocent souls – were being fingerprinted not more than a crosswalk away. Of course, during the early afternoon, most of the detainees brought into the department are mentally ill street people. If you're interested in appreciating the tragicomic tale that is humanity, about 1 p.m. is the time to come. In those first hours after lunch, the department becomes a circus train of schizophrenia, obsessive compulsion and the vainglorious flights of bipolar disorder in full bloom. It's as heartrending as it is morbidly fascinating.

After a 72-hour psych evaluation (the longest they can hold you against your will), offenders will likely receive a diagnosis that no agency in the county of Sonoma is capable of handling. So, the crazies are back on the street until they do something offensive enough to warrant another arrest. Nudity helps.

The station was exceptionally clean and smelled like it was recently rinsed in a lemon-scented chemical bath.

I approached the counter and spoke to the woman behind the glass. She was cheery in a manner that threw me off. Then she answered the phone and mowed the poor soul on the other end with the kind of bureaucratic bellicoso that only comes with years of institutionalized not-giving-a-fuck.

"Detective Shane, please," I said.

"Hold on, I'll get her." She smiled. Having seen and heard her phone-persona in action, I waited for her to flip on me. Never came.

I sat next to an ashen man in a brown suit who reeked of burnt coffee or pee. He clutched a briefcase with a handle he had home-repaired with a wad of duct tape, blackened where his sweaty grip had worked in its grime. On the wall opposite were posters of missing children. Some of the kids had been gone for years and had older-looking images Photoshopped next to their once-cherubic faces. I wondered who did the age progression, failed art students who'd drifted into forensics? Or was it all done by a computer now, and did the parents ever ask for prints for their wallets? Macabre thoughts came to me on deadline – the first sputters of the story engine cranking back to life.

Between the posters of the kids were notices for someone called Professor Alexandria Ashe who had likewise disappeared to the two-dimensional Phantom Zone of color copies. Ashe was a striking grey-blonde cougar with hairpin eyebrows, who had gone missing (or on the lam) about a month ago.

"She's popular," I said to the man in the brown suit and pointed to the half-dozen likenesses of the missing woman that surrounded us.

The man in the brown suit propped his briefcase atop his knees and drummed the sides as his eyes skittered from me to the woman behind the glass. He was afraid of her and my chatter was making him nervous.

There was a loud buzz and the brown suit clutched his briefcase to his chest. The woman behind the glass motioned for me to enter the door adjacent to the window.

"I guess I'm up," I said to the suit.

"Oh, yes, yes, of course, it's you," he said. A sad note grew in his voice with each successive word. "I'm not here to see anyone."

The dude was there on spec. Or at least Thorazine.

* * *

Over the workstation of the woman behind the glass I could see Detective Shane through the blinds in her office. She was more attractive than I remembered. New pantsuit and a recent visit to a nail salon, I surmised. I'd heard her joke at the crime scene that inhaling the fumes at her salon was the only legal way she could get high. I caught her eye. She waved. She was talking to someone and her gestures looked like she was carving the air with her nails. I couldn't hear her through the bulletproof glass.

She looked back at me, perplexed.

Detective Shane stood and opened her blinds completely. I could see into the office now. She was talking to a boy, a preteen, maybe ten, maybe more. He nodded when our eyes briefly met. Detective Shane gestured for me to join her and opened the door as I approached.

"He thought he recognized you," she said, a hand on his narrow shoulder. She turned to the boy. "This is Daedalus Howell, he's a reporter for..." she let her voice trail diplomatically, unsure of present employment status. "He writes for newspapers."

I coughed.

The kid brushed a dark lock off his cheek and narrowed his sea-green eyes at me. I thought to myself that if he asks what a newspaper is, I'm gonna slap him. Detective Shane knelt to the kid's eye-level, which broke the gaze he had fixed on me since I'd walked in. "Is Mr. Howell a friend of your parents?"

He just stared. Then finally shook his head. Detective Shane sighed and said, "Meet John Doe. He won't tell me his name."

I extended my hand but he just stared at his shoes – a pair of licorice-black hush puppies that looked standard issue with his navy blue school uniform and white oxford shirt. The blazer was what I remembered from the incident, due to the ostentatious patch on the breast pocket. From a distance it looked like an old Cadillac emblem but close up it was a gold shield surrounded by a semi-circle of laurel leaves like the kind you see on film fest posters.

"You two should get along. Got the same fashion sense," Detective Shane laughed and then thought that perhaps she had offended me until I mustered a chuckle.

I was preoccupied with the kid, who looked familiar, damn near archetypal, like a kid from a TV commercial. Not the plucky hooligan in the detergent ad with the trifecta of grass, mud and blood staining his jeans, but the classy car commercial kid who looks pensively out the rear window admiring the curves of the verdant roadside – that kid.

His hair was a deep chestnut and he was biscuit-colored, probably more genetics than sun, though the UV rays certainly helped. No freckles, just a small constellation of small, dark moles above his dimples. Given how coiffed he was, his blazer made him look a little like a ventriloquist's dummy.

"Learn something everyday," Detective Shane said.

He looked about to speak but hesitated.

"All he would say is that he's in the wrong place," she added. "But we have no reports of missing children in the entire state, he's got no prints on file, no identification whatsoever. But somebody obviously takes good care of him. His jacket cost more than your entire wardrobe."

She might've been right.

"Just walked in here saying he was lost but his address is local. Well, it looks local until you try to find it on Google Maps, which says it doesn't exist. I had an officer waste an hour of your taxpayer dollars just to make sure," she said.

I looked at the kid and snapped my fingers to get his

attention.

"You don't know your own address?"

"I told her my address. She just can't find it."

"Either he's got the wrong address or he's insane. But he doesn't look insane," said Shane.

"Looks can be deceiving."

"True that," she said.

"Why won't you tell her your name, kid?" I asked. I tried to sound friendly but I was out of practice.

Shane leaned toward him and pouted.

"Are you in trouble? Is that why you don't want to tell us who you are?" she asked, a kind of maternal note rising in her voice. The boy shrugged and the tailored shoulders of his blazer rose and fell with perfect symmetry. Given the cost of private school, it seemed somebody, somewhere cared about this jerk, or at least wanted to look like they cared.

"Who did you think Mr. Howell was?" Shane asked. The question snapped me out of my own thoughts.

The boy shrugged again, then half-assed, "My teacher." He was improvising.

"What school do you go to?"

"James Schow Memorial School...." he began but, muttered the rest as if ashamed. I couldn't make it out. Shane could.

She raised her eyebrows as if impressed as she repeated "... for Gifted Children," then chided, "That at least checks out – it's on the patch on the breast pocket. You're a helluva detective, Daedalus."

At the mention of my name, the boy shook his head and repeated it under his breath like a curse word. I didn't like it when people gave me grief about my name, let alone a kid.

"So, whose jacket is this?" I asked, and before Shane could say not to, I grabbed his lapel and turned it to reveal the pocket on the inside – where I'd keep my reporter's notebook. There was an embroidered patch with the tailor's insignia on it. There, block-printed in a careful hand, was the name "Jude."

He pulled away.

"Are you Jude or did you just steal his jacket?"

Jude stared at his shoes.

"You get a point for that," Shane said to me. "But it's a dead end. "I looked up the school. Emailed his picture – nada. No one recognizes him." She turned to the kid.

"Can you tell Mr. Howell what happened to you, Jude?"

"I told you. I got off the bus from school and was walking home. I went to my block and turned the corner and my house wasn't there," he said with an exasperated puff. The way he kneaded his palm with his knuckles told me he was scared but he fronted well.

"Clearly you were on the wrong block."

"No, I wasn't. I know my way around town. I got here didn't I?"

Detective Shane corroborated the fact that the boy had strolled into the police station of his own accord, for which she took pains to applaud him. "If more kids knew where to go when they were in trouble, this would be a happier city."

"So, what, is this like an amnesia thing?" I asked Shane, then asked the kid, "Do you remember getting hit on the head or anything?"

"How could I remember getting hit on the head if I have amnesia?"

Detective Shane clucked her tongue.

"So, I'm ready to go now," Jude said to me as if it were a foregone conclusion that I was his ride.

"Kid, you don't even know where your house is. Also, I'm not a taxi driver. Or a teacher," I said and turned to Shane.

"Okay, thanks for the freak show. I'm gonna go."

She nodded, trying to hide her apathy. I looked back at the kid and said, "You know, when I was your age, they had a saying, 'Just say no.'" Detective Shane rolled her eyes. "Next time someone offers you whatever you're on, now you know what to say."

I opened the office door and stepped out. Before the door swept behind me, the kid was on his feet.

"Fergus! Wait!" he called from the other side of the glass.

I felt like someone had shinned me with a railroad tie. Then I was angry. I pivoted and swung the door open and caught the kid as he tumbled forward. I pegged a finger to his chest and glowered at him, waiting for the right words to come, but they didn't.

Everyone has a name on their list that will stop them in their tracks upon hearing it. Sometimes it's an enemy, a former lover, someone to whom one owes money – whatever. That name, for me, was "Kit Fergus."

How the kid somehow knew that particular name was only a secondary consideration in that moment. What was working me over in my mind was who it belonged to – or, at least used to belong to. Namely, so to speak, me.

* * *

"Is this some kind of a fucking joke?" I said, astonished as I heard the words, singed with ire, rage from my mouth. The boy looked genuinely scared for a moment. Detective Shane pulled Jude to her side and raised an eyebrow at me.

"He touch a nerve, Dade?"

"Sorry. It's just a coincidence, I suppose. Statistically impossible, but probably just..."

"What are you not telling me here?"

I pulled Detective Shane into the corner of her office and

spoke softly as Jude F. did his best poker face.

"That name..."

"Mm-hmm?" came from Shane like an accusation.

"Well, you know how some writers use pseudonyms for their bylines?"

"I know where this is going."

I second-guessed her.

"Kit Fergus is not my pseudonym, Detective Shane."

"Honey, no one is born into this world named 'Daedalus Howell.' So, what's up with Kit Fergus? You moonlighting?"

Jude had sat himself in Detective Shane's chair. Her blue sweater rested over the chair such that it looked like a cape behind the kid's shoulders.

"He's Kit Fergus," Jude F. said as he began to swivel the chair.

"That so?"

"No. Well, yes, in a way. It was my original name."

"You his teacher? 'Cuz, if you're that boy's teacher you better take him home to his parents and get this bullshit out of my life before I have to write it up," she said. Then she looked me dead in the eye. "Are you his daddy?"

"No! Hell, no," I said, perhaps a tad too fast.

"Grandfather?"

"Now you're just being rude."

Detective Shane set her jaw as she concentrated for a moment. Finally, she said, "Listen, if you're a blood relative and there's some kind of personal, family situation going on but you can act as a legal guardian – I suggest that you do."

"I'm not," I said. "This kid is some kind of clever con-man. In fact, you'd better be sure he isn't some kind of midget super-villain."

Detective Shane looked hard at Jude.

"You a midget super-villain?"

"I'm not a midget, I'm just a little undersized for my age because I was born premature. I'm eleven."

"That's when it usually starts," I said.

"You still here?" she asked me, then raised her finger, a long, acrylic fingernail extension coming off it like a crescent moon. She pointed to the door. Jude glared at me as I walked out.

"You're the only person I know!" he yelled as the heavy glass door closed and muffled his voice.

He'll be fine, I thought to myself. A kid as canny as that would fly through the psychiatric exam, easily outwitting the student shrink saddled with the gig. Then he could charm his new foster parents out of their life savings. Given the amount those people are compensated, that would be about sixty bucks. Just enough for a new video game, I thought. The sooner they start, the longer the con. I'd seen it before – when I was his age, when I was just like him. Almost made me take a shine to the kid, but then I'm no sap. Well, that's what Philip Marlowe would say at least. More to the point, this kid wasn't going to be my career-redeeming story.

Or at least that's what I thought then.

6.
Happy Birthday, Mr. McCormack

All that ballyhoo at the police station had cost me valuable time and if I was going to file something on the centenarian before he died it was going to have to be soon. I wasn't the only one with concerns about his longevity. My phone vibrated and I fished it from my pocket. Adriane texted me: "100 bday Chprl Hse Brk 300 wrs +pic b4 ded."

I immediately replied "On it!" and then thought how Mssrs. Broca and Wernicke had never anticipated that the language centers of the brain would be used to decode such abysmal communication. After meditating on the notion for several minutes, aided by Google's "*Did you mean...?*" search help, I decoded Adriane's telegraphic missive to mean she wanted me pen a 300-word human interest piece on a centenarian at Chaparral House in Lumaville to be filed prior to his or her death – with a picture to boot. Sure. I was grateful for the assignment but I couldn't help wonder which of the interns had turned it down.

Adriane hadn't bothered to tell me the name of my interviewee, so I figured I'd chance it. Besides, I'm sure Adriane didn't know his name either, and revealing my ignorance was second only to revealing hers. I couldn't afford to piss her off as I noticed I'd been sliding down the pole a bit in terms of beats. It seemed my new beat was just a tic left of the "human interest" stories to which I'd grown accustomed. Lately, it'd been the crackpots, weirdos and malcontents in the ultraviolet spectrum of our local color.

I used to be on the arts and entertainment beat, but that space became overrun with celebrity gossip and other crap fed automatically by content farms. Wine also evaporated as a dependable source of revenue (as well as free wine) when everyone under the Tuscan sun became a wine blogger. Then beer bloggers, then Belgian ale bloggers, and then, and then, and then... Elevate any socially-acceptable vice to "artisanal" status and some asshole already has a Twitter account on it with a half-a-million followers.

So, I kept moving into stranger and stranger territory, looking for leads that were geographically specific to me and the few of my colleagues who could stroll the blocks. Smart, eh? Hyperlocal – one might think this would limit the readership to, say, one's apartment building. However, the trick was to find the "universal in the esoteric," the common humanity that united us all, you know, under our tinfoil hats.

One would assume that my habitues between San Francisco and Lumaville would provide no dearth of material. Wrong. Most of the eccentrics one finds roaming the open streets A) live there and B) will not suffer the indignity of an interview, especially when they make me for a CIA agent or, worse, a missionary. I attribute this misperception to the fact that I wear a sport coat everywhere as part of my "action figure" ensemble. By "action figure" ensemble I mean the ubiquitous uniform they'll mold into an action figure when I'm rich and famous. And more to the point, I didn't want to exploit the disenfranchised and mentally ill who comprise my beat's population. And my readers.

* * *

I parked the Mini mid-block on Hayes Street, a quick jog from the Chaparral House. The roofline of the place looked as though its architect was drawing a triangle, got bored halfway through and tried to cover the unfinished line with shingles. If the architect didn't give a shit, the gardener did, tracing the sprawl of the institutional grounds with tiny flowers, meticulously arranged, as if it were a massive funeral plot.

I cut across the sprawling lawn and onto a brick patio. A vinyl awning, yellowed with age, flapped in the breeze. The door was open.

Inside, it wasn't difficult to locate the birthday boy. Chaparral House looked as though the Hallmark factory had exploded inside it. Rainbow-colored streamers clung to the ceiling like spider webs, and banners that read "Happy Birthday" and "Happy 100, Mac!" lined the halls. A flock of handmade cards pasted and colored by children from a local school stuck to the walls like candy-colored moths. In a corner, a grand bouquet of helium balloons hovered, waiting it seemed, to levitate some oldster into the wild blue yonder.

Underlying all the gaiety was a stiff whiff of chemistry. I assumed it was disinfectants used to clean the damp couches, but then I realized it was medicine. Not the pills and potions themselves, but the reek wafting from the glue factory of elderly bodies.

"Better dying through chemistry," I muttered.

Just beyond the door was a small bureau helmed by a dark, middle-aged woman with close-cropped hair. She cleared her throat.

She had the Zen-like mien one might expect of someone who oversees a depot to the afterlife. She was cutting paper dolls into a wad of burgundy tissue paper. She glanced up at me, smiled, and returned to her scissoring.

I approached the paper doll lady as she unfolded an accordion of miniature women, each one a perfect clone of its sister.

"Is the celebrity centenarian in the house?" I said. I can be cute like that.

Her eyes bounced off my new jacket, then hovered on my face a second.

"I'm a reporter," I said as I pulled out my reporter's notebook to sell it better. No bogus insurance policies or title deeds here. She decided I was legit, or at least incapable of defrauding an old person. I needed to get a smarter coat.

"Mr. McCormack is in number 209. Down West Hall, odd numbers on the left-hand side," she said. "Now, you should know, that he has what they call Reduplicative paramnesia. He thinks he's here but he's really there, if you know what I mean." She fanned her paper dolls in the air to indicate the beyond.

* * *

The term "convalescent home" always seemed a bit of a charade to me. No one goes to convalesce so much as to wait for the inevitable with such farcical distractions such as bridge and a woman who comes to play piano on Tuesdays. Perhaps, I've got the whole thing backwards and these people are convalescing, that is, doing their best to recover from their misspent youths. I might have to do the same before hiding my face among a crowd of stars.

I shuffled down the hall past a menagerie of Time's

ravaged trophies. A woman in a wheelchair was rolled within spitting distance of a blaring flat-screen television. A daytime talk show host was outing some poor schmuck's lurid kink to his wife. Nearby, a grizzled old dude in a plaid jacket was loudly complaining about the quality of his thermos. He was holding a plastic water bottle.

In a room off the main hall, seated octogenarians waved their arms in the air like sea anemones, goaded by an energetic young woman in a purple leotard. I caught her eye as we strolled passed the door and was impressed by the warmth of her smile. I figured her for a volunteer on a account of the purple, which, in my experience, meant she was some kind of secular nun, a notion that might sound oxymoronic were it not for the preponderance of piety that afflicted some women in their 20s in the twilight between graduation and their first non-profit gig.

I rounded the corner into a residential wing. On each door was a plastic green medallion dangling from a hook. On each was engraved the phrase "I'm OK." The old people put them out every morning so the staff knows they're alive. No sign meant a room is for rent.

I knocked on the door at 209. Nothing. I knocked again. Nothing. I cleared my throat and knocked a little harder.

Still nothing.

I fished my phone out of my pocket and thought about what I should text to Adriane – some bullshit like "100 = DOA. Sry." Her reply, I imagined, would be "UR frd."

"Whatever you're selling, I ain't buying," a raspy voice muttered behind me. Though the old man's upper-plate had certainly seen better days, it had surely seen its share of shit-eating. He was holding a slice of birthday cake on a plastic plate, the lip of which had cracked from the tremor in his spotted hand.

"Mac?" I asked as I stepped out of the way.

"100 fucking years and they get me a sheet cake from a grocery store," he grumbled as he lifted a key to the lock. It was clear he wasn't going to get the key in the keyhole until his next birthday, so I offered help. He batted me away.

"What they don't tell you here is that it's the same key for every room," he said. "That's only a problem if you go to the wrong door. You're liable to get in and start living another man's life. Of course, their wives don't seem to mind." He winked and shimmied into his room.

7.

Dewey Wins

Jimmy McCormack was a dapper old gent whose enthusiasm for straw hats and seersucker jackets belied the fashion sense of another era. Sometime between World War I and II, I figured. The man was ancient but refreshingly sharp and didn't look a day over 80. Rather, after a certain point, you just can't tell how the hell old someone is anymore. You can either see their skull or not, right?

He was thin and tall and still had a full head of hair, which suggested more vitality than one might expect from someone containing a century's worth of experience.

The room, on the other hand, was practically the opposite of Mac's otherwise composed demeanor. It was small and dark and smelled of cooking grease and air-freshener, the kind found in cars – gooey and tropical. Heavy blinds blocked most of the light. Mac had traded the sun for a gaudy lamp that glowed orange through its shade across a card table that seemed to be the center of his activity. There was a mess of dirty plates, unopened mail and a day planner calendar on which he had exed out all the days theretofore. On this particular day he had written "100" followed by "-63" for some reason.

"Happy birthday Mac."

"That's what they tell me."

"I'm just here for some quotes."

"How many of you paperboys are coming by today?" he asked with a smile. "That's how we used to talk in the newsroom back in my day."

"You were a newspaperman?"

Mac motioned for us to sit down but the furniture was rather scarce. We crowded around the card table.

"I was a newspaperman back when we still had newspapers," he said. "No offense."

Oh, crap, here's comes the "back in my day" lecture. Last thing I needed was a history lesson that was going to exceed my word count. Still, watching someone that old in action had its own points of fascination. I imagined it was kind of like being a marine biologist and stumbling across a coelacanth, which was thought to have gone extinct in the Late Cretaceous until they found one swimming off the coast of South Africa. Now, here was one eating sheet cake.

I took out my phone and launched my voice recording app.

"You mind if I record some quotes?"

"You want me to talk into the thingamajig? Eggs in the coffee," he smiled, which I took to mean it was alright.

"Where did you work?" I asked.

"Everywhere but mostly in Chicago at the Trib. I was a reporter most of my 30s. That used to be middle-aged, you know. Now they got all these vitamins and boner pills. It's how you can be alive and a stiff at the same time," he said and started to laugh but stifled it for fear of mortal injury. "Anyway, it was a long time ago."

"Break any big stories?" I asked, realizing my 300 word puff piece was already going nowhere. A centenarian speaking about Viagra might have legs – three, in fact, but

I was breaking the first rule of human interest stories – don't get interested in the human. You're liable to end up in a conversation and later have to fish through endless yammering for a few salient soundbites. Not only does this bring down your hourly rate by increasing the hours relative to the horseshit-per-word fee, it can become expensive if, like me, you use a transcriber app.

Unfortunately, there's no artificial intelligence smart enough to parse whatever the hell it is people are saying through the slur of accents that inhibit effective transcription by machine. But there are emerging economies. Once my interview is recorded, the app beams it into the cloud, where a typist in Bangalore, the Philippines or even Lumaville's east side does the work sifting words from white noise. Essentially, I've outsourced my carpal tunnel syndrome.

The app charges a penny a word, meaning that the dude in Bangalore is getting only a percentage of that per word, which someday, my rate will probably become as well. Problems start when I get some loquacious motherfucker riled up and talking. Suddenly, twenty minutes is 4,000 words and I'm sending $40 to the Far East. I wasn't sure how much of my money Mac might send the people of the Republic of India but I instantly regretted asking "Break any big stories?"

Mac leaned back in his chair and gave me a stern look.

"No. I didn't break shit."

I was caught off guard. "No?"

"Not really, no."

The irony. At this rate, my transcriber was going to starve. And so was I.

"There must be something you're proud of," I asked, faking collegial bon homme.

"How long you been on the beat, son?"

Enough said. I understood what he was getting at –

sometimes the birdcage liner was always birdcage liner.

"Well, you going to answer my question?" he prodded. I didn't realize he was serious.

"15 years – give or take."

"In that time, you ever write a story where you thought you had all the facts, everything was pointing to a single, simple conclusion but then – blammo!" Mac exclaimed, wildly waving his arms. He then closed his eyes and slowly said, as if to savor it, "Dewey wins."

* * *

It took me a moment to understand what he was saying. Too long for Mac's taste. He repeated "Dewey wins" with extra emphasis on the syllables as if I were deaf.

It all came back.

One humid Spring day at Lumaville State when the j-school lecture caught my attention long enough to glance away from the thighs of the girl next to me. It was a case study in second-guessing reality and anticipating what you think might be news before it is.

"No, fucking way. You wrote 'Dewey Wins?'" I said.

A twinkle sparked from Mac's upper plate. He could tell I was impressed. But would Adriane the Editrix be impressed? Would she even know what I was talking about?

It goes like this: "Dewey Defeats Truman" is the infamous headline printed on the front page of the November 3, 1948 Chicago Tribune, after then-President Truman beat his Republican rival Governor Thomas Dewey of New York for the presidency. The Trib figured Dewey for a lock and got ahead of themselves with the printing press. That would never happen today. Once hip to the error, Adriane or her clone would upload a correction faster than one could say "Google cache."

I once saw a parody of "Dewey Defeats Truman" in which a smiling Jesus held a newspaper that read "Death Defeats Jesus." It must have been post-resurrection, I figured. His lawyer should've demanded a retraction, but obviously, his lawyer was shit.

Dewey wins.

This could be a magazine story, I thought – the man who wrote the wrongest headline ever. Perhaps I should tell Adriane that her lead had died and make off with the quotes. If I could land a mag story or at least get mag rates I could catch up on the Mini Cooper payments, which were beginning to pile (the Golden Star Credit Union had a nasty collector who liked to remind me).

* * *

Mac steadied himself on the card table as he rose from his chair, then shuffled over to a bookshelf that looked like a tenement for National Geographic magazines.

"Son, could you get that hatbox over there?" On the bottom shelf was an octagonal-shaped box of thick cardboard. I lurched it off the shelf and let it thud onto the card table.

"What's in there, your bowling ball?" I asked.

"Proof," Mac said with a snarl.

"You don't have to prove it to me, Mac."

Mac shook the lid off the box with his trembling hands sending a plume of dust eddying into the still air of his room. Then he became very still. Even his hands momentarily lost their tremor as he slowly reached into the box and exhumed an ancient broadsheet. It was brown with age and looked like it had been steeped in tea.

"I mean, it's true that Dewey won," he said.

Shit. The old man was crazy. Of course, Dewey had lost and now I was losing too. Like the scissor lady said, "reduplicative paramnesia."

I laughed to ease the tension, which just made it more tense.

"You're saying that Give 'Em Hell Harry didn't win the election?" I asked hesitantly.

"He sure as hell didn't win," Mac said.

"Neither did George W. Bush but he still got to live in the White House for eight years," I replied. "Listen, Mac, newspaperman to newspaperman – I don't need a conspiracy story, I need 250 words that use the keyword phrase 'how to live to a hundred' enough times to achieve optimal density."

"You don't believe me. I don't expect you to believe me. But you might appreciate this..."

Mac handed me another brittle newspaper from the hat box. It was another old paper – from the following day. Mac's hands were trembling again but this time from anger.

Mac huffed and looked through the slim vista of his blinds. Outside, a man and his son, a kid about Jude's age, crossed a cement courtyard that doubled as the staff smoking area. It made me think that if Jude were a better con artist, he too would be here, doing his lost boy routine for stale saltines, sticks of gum and the occasional annuity check.

"November 3, 1948," Mac muttered.

I unfolded the newspaper and laid it flat, gently, like putting down a sleeping baby. I scanned it. Where I had expected to read a mea culpa and editors falling over themselves with retractions, I instead read "Dewey Starts Choosing Cabinet" and "President-Elect Dewey Meets with Truman."

"Now how do you explain that?" He squinted hard at me. I squinted back. It took a moment but my skepticism came back like a flush to the cheeks. Had I stumbled onto the longest con in history? Or...

"About a week after President Dewey was elected I went on a assignment to the University of Chicago physics department. Some slide-rule type had a breakthrough he was desperate to share before the government funding was gone. He was a charlatan so far as I could tell, or at least misguided enough that he at least fooled himself. He had this machine, see..."

* * *

I could always tell when the bullshit machine was being cranked up. You develop a nose for it when you're on the crackpot beat. The dispossessed have nothing to say so they say the most, building castles in the air only to claim the tragedy of their stony ruin. This beat had given me my fill of other people's bullshit. The lonely bluster, the sad inventions, the losing dreams – I'd come to hate their harbingers because I feared I was becoming one of them.

I gave Mac a taste of my professional snark.

"Was this machine a printing press? Did it print novelty newspapers?" I said with a haughty laugh. "I gotta guy who sends me my own obituary every week. It's a gag, man. People make fake news, put their own pictures next to a humongous fish or write 'Man bites dog' in twenty-point type across four columns because they're assholes who never rate a real story. I came here to write about a birthday party, not a prop comedy act."

Mac stood up. His fists were two tight, white tennis balls. He slammed a fist into the hatbox, knocking it off the coffee table. Tea-yellow sheets sifted to the linoleum floor and piled like autumn leaves.

The old man and I stood looking at the mess. Chivalry got the better of me. I sighed and dropped to my good knee to collect Mac's reliquary of news that never happened. In so doing, I noticed that each paper was dated sequentially and each referenced President Dewey.

"You call that a comedy show, partner?" he said. "I ain't laughing."

The blog had gone out the window. Adriane and the search engine robots that enslaved us could give a crap about some delusional century-old shyster who had forgotten that the novelty editions he owned weren't actually real. They probably weren't even old, but rather the pride and joy of some amateur propsmith on eBay. Perhaps that's the angle, I thought. How oldsters get conned by fake antiques from fictional pasts.

"If you live to be a hundred, and by the looks of you, you won't, you see a lot of strange shit," he said. "You drink?"

I frowned at my boots. Mac nodded – he had me. My company was easily bought, at this rate of production I wouldn't be buying my own drinks at the bar after long.

Mac ambled to the kitchen.

"There was this machine at the U. The paper sent me there. It was to be some sort of cheerleading piece about our advancements in military science or some crock," he said as he fetched a pair of tumblers decorated with racist cartoon characters from a long-defunct restaurant.

"It was some kinda device, not a weapon per se, but a kind of trump card they considered using during the Korean War," he said as he put a glass in front of me. It had two fingers of scotch, neat. I took a slug, a little too quickly. Mac's glass was in mid-toast as I swallowed a burning peat bog coal. He just shook his head and let his eyes grow far away. A little too far for my taste. I leaned heavily upon the rickety card table to rattle him back to life. I wasn't the only person thinking this way.

A fireplug in a nurse's uniform poked her head in and advised we'd have five more minutes before Mac would have to rest.

"If you let him, he'll keep you all day long," she said as she entered and proceeded to fluff any pillow she could get her pudgy hands on. I expected her to conclude with a knowing smile, but it never came. She just shook her wide, dark-haired head and repeated, "Five more minutes. And that's it."

Mac shuddered. I couldn't tell if he was playing or was really chilled by the nurse. I had a feeling he couldn't tell either. "The irony," he muttered. "You wait sixty years to tell a story and they give you five minutes to do it. Is that thing on?" he gestured to my phone.

"Yes, the whole time," I said, doing my part for developing nations.

"Good. Let's finally put Looking Glass on the record. The story I wrote back in the day got cut to the bone, at least in this edition," he said with a wink, then fished the pile of newspapers on the floor and pulled up a single sheet. Then he tore a palm-sized selection from it. I heard myself gasp.

"Take it," he said, the clip wafting in the breeze like a feather. I must have still looked astonished that he so cavalierly tore into his precious archive. Fake or not. "It's just fish wrap," he chided.

"That's some old fish," I said. "Like a coelacanth." There's that word again.

I began to read Mac's clip but he waved his hands like an impatient kid, so I rolled the scrap around my pen like a novice trying to roll a joint. I put it in my pocket for safekeeping.

"What did the machine do?" he asked himself. "Nothing. Not a goddamn thing. Or, so it seemed at the time. It was like the guy flipped on the light switch but there was no juice. Nothing happened. I forget the fellow's name, odd duck, shifty. It's in the clip."

I made a half-hearted reach to my pocket but Mac stopped me. I went for the tumbler instead.

"You do your homework later. Here's the jist before Flo Nightengale gets back. Looking Glass doesn't officially exist. It was a Korean War thing. The thinking went, I suppose, coming after World War Two that they had to top the atom bomb. This this was supposed to be different. Still physics, but no bang, no boom," Mac said. "Tactically speaking, it wasn't even a weapon so much as a means of re-aligning..."

He paused, looked puzzled, then I realized he had caught his own reflection in a small-framed mirror on the wall above where I was sitting.

"Re-aligning what?" I asked.

"What we know as reality. They thought they were working on time travel or some such nonsense. At least that's what I gleaned that day. But it was something else. They ended up with something entirely different and they made me their guinea pig."

"How so? You said they just flipped a switch and nothing happened," I reminded.

"Nothing happened, that time," he said. "When the clip came out, the Professor wasn't too happy about it. Nothing bad about him, just not enough of him. I explained that there were these assholes called editors but, you know. I offered to buy the Professor a drink after work and he accepted. Asked me to meet him at the lab. I tucked a few editions in a valise and was on my way."

I made a mental note – never meet a professor after hours

in a lab.

"I meet the man up there. Same crew as before," Mac continued. "Said they were going to try the experiment again. He flipped a switch. Nothing happened. But everything had happened. I didn't notice at first. There was just subtle differences. Like those puzzles in the B section with the two look-alike drawings and you gotta find the five things that are different between the two. Everything was suddenly like that. A guy's tie was different, the secretary was suddenly wearing glasses – the kind of thing that you don't notice until you do," Mac said. "It's unconscious at first, you ignore it. Then some things you can't ignore."

"Like what?"

"Like an empty glass," he said with a smile. The cork squeaked from its bottle and Mac poured me another couple of knuckles' worth. I wasn't moving anyway but it kept me there all the same.

"Then Enoch's disappeared," he said. "My favorite watering hole after work. It just up and disappeared."

"It disappeared?"

"More like it never existed," he said with that faraway look again. "Thought I was on the wrong street. Nope, I was where it was supposed to be. But sure as shit, it wasn't there. Same but different when I got to my apartment. Looked like home, but it wasn't home."

I let the words hang for a moment. I realized there was no point disagreeing with him. Besides, it was his birthday and there was at least a quarter bottle left.

"And that's how I got here. Not the home, but Lumaville," he said.

Lumaville, of course, where all the nuts end up. He leaned forward.

"In Chicago, I went back to the lab to find the sonofabitch who flipped the switch. Not a trace."

"He split?"

"He never existed. I was in the wrong place, why would he? If Enoch's was gone and goddamn Ike was president – who knows where the guy went."

"To Lumaville?" I had to try.

"In a manner of speaking, yes. His work did. Some wingdings opened up an FBI file in the 1960s. They were part of a physics club here at the U. Working on wormholes, parallel universes, your basic hippie shit."

"So, what did you do?"

Mac smiled and sat back. I'm sure he thought I was another in a long line of assholes who told him he had lost his last marble.

"Let me try something on you."

"Fair enough."

"You're dreaming – dreaming you're being chased by a tiger. It's gnashing its teeth, it's on your heels, you know any minute that it's going to bite you in the ass. You also know you're dreaming. What do you do?"

A zen puzzle. I always hated this kind of rhetorical bullshit because I always got it wrong.

Old guys were always pulling this nonsense on me because I've got the kind of face that says I think I'm smart. It's mostly my nose.

"Well, if I knew I was dreaming," I began, "I'd turn around and confront the tiger, then I'd –"

"Why don't you just wake the fuck up? If you know you're dreaming, just wake the fuck up."

"Got it," I said and finished my drink.

Mac shook his head and put his hundred-year-old hands on his knees. I thought they looked gnarled, but no more so than those of someone in their 70s, say. I wouldn't know. Age didn't really show on him. Perhaps after he croaked, they'd slice up his brain and count the rings like it was some petrified redwood.

"Now me, I can't wake up. I just learned to accept. This is where I am. I was old then and I'm older now. Comes to a point when you just have to live your life again – wherever it is. I met a girl, had a kid..."

I was not impressed with how the story was tying up and he could tell.

"What? Not enough of an ending for ya?"

I had to prevent myself from involuntarily shaking my head. Mac sighed.

"You got kids?"

"No," I said.

"Damn shame. Your abstract troubles are meaningless when the boogeyman is out. Perspective," he said.

Warmth buzzed through my body like a low current of electricity. The scotch was doing its trick. I waited for the sedative ease, but it didn't come. Instead, I felt a thwack to my eyebrow. It was my own palm flat against my face. Sometimes the body knows what the brain is trying get to first. Jude. The little con artist. I stood up and nearly toppled the card table.

"You're not going to believe me..." I said.

"It's okay, you don't believe me, so we're even."

"No, listen, you're the second person I've spoken to today that's gone through this."

"This what?"

"Being in the wrong place," I said.

Mac screwed up his face as if to show he knew I was winding him up.

"Is that so?"

"There was this kid. There was a shooting, but never mind that – at the police station, later we're both there because..."

"You shot a kid?" Mac joked as he reached for the bottle.

"Listen, the kid had no ID, no parents, nothing but this elaborate story about getting off the bus and his house wasn't there," I said. "What's weird is that there's no record of this kid anywhere. No school records, no birth certificate. Nothing. It's like he..."

The bottle smashed on the floor. I reeled back from the crash and splashed scotch on my new coat. This is why I wear black.

Mac was still. His hand was open but motionless like a mannequin's.

"It was like he arrived out of nowhere wasn't it?" he said. His eyes were in the mirror again. Then they were on me with a fierceness that made me sit.

"You gotta help this kid! You gotta get him back where he belongs and find the sonofabitch who did this!" he yelled. "It's your responsibility as a newspaperman..." The words sputtered out. Mac slumped in his chair.

Something beeped. I looked at the phone, having forgotten I was recording, but that wasn't it. I looked at Mac. He was wasn't moving. The beeping was coming from his shirt pocket. I rushed to him, but by the time I reached his chair, the fireplug nurse and a lanky sidekick were in the door.

"Don't touch him!" the nurse commanded.

I backed away as a smile creased Mac's blue-grey lips. His eyelids shuddered open and his milky eyes shone clear and sharp. The nurses fluttered around him like pigeons. They heaved him into a wheelchair and started rolling him out of the room.

"Where are you taking him?" I asked.

Over the beeping of his alarm, Mac managed, "To the waters and the wild..."

The nurses turned the corner with enough speed that the alarm had a Doppler effect as they sped down the hall.

I turned off the recording app.

* * *

Later, down the hall, Nurse Fireplug was waiting for the coffee machine to finish a new pot. She slouched against the countertop, the fluorescent tube of the lights comically reflecting in her glasses like neon eyebrows. She saw me pass the doorway.

"Capgras syndrome," she said just before the coffee machine belched out the last of its brew. "That's what they say he has."

"Is he going to make it?"

"Boy, he's a hundred years old," she said. "They haven't cured that shit yet."

"What's Capgras syndrome?"

"Reduplicative paramnesia."

"I knew it."

"Makes you think that you're in the wrong place. Or that everything and everyone around you has been replaced with a double," she said and gestured to the coffee pot. I nodded and she pulled a paper cup from the stack. "You take anything?"

I shrugged and the nurse poured a cup of black coffee.

"The brain starts to make up stories to explain it and then you start believing your own bullshit. That's what gets you."

The coffee was surprisingly good and I needed it more than I realized.

"It's nice of you to take the time," she said. "He's outlived everyone else in his life."

"I thought he said he had a kid," I said between sips.

The nurse frowned and shook her head. "Nope. Not that

I'm aware of. There's no next-of-kin on his paperwork. But, you see, that's the kind of thing he would say, you know?"

I nodded, thanked the nurse for the coffee. I made my way through the wide corridors, occasionally greeted by a stray oldster.

"Just wake up," I thought. "Just wake the fuck up."

8.
Inverting Pyramids

Back in J-school, we were taught ye olde "inverted pyramid" model of news writing. Put the important bits up top and continue downward with decreasing relevance to the bottom. That way, whom ever was doing paste-up could trim from the bottom if your piece didn't fit or wasn't going to jump.

This was before the web offered us an infinite canvas on which to paint our portraits of humanity, which is ironic since we use so little of it. A couple hundred words is apparently where the human attention span begins to wane. Somebody tested it – a gig so boring, I could only imagine that their attention waned first and they cut the test short to go watch paint dry somewhere.

I didn't learn the modern mode of coverage until my tour of duty at the blog factory, which was known in what remained of the industry for both for its systematic degradation of the language and its uncanny ability to build vast readerships on the shallowest of concepts. The relationship between the content makers and the content consumers could be succinctly summed by Ben Kenobi: "Who's more foolish – the fool or the fool who follows him?"

At the blog factory, our procedure was based on appeasing both search engine robots and our readers, who were in search of the diverting snark we mutually pretended was news. All coverage began not with the question "what's happening?" but "what's trending?"

There are a number of ways to gauge this – the most useful being an upstream gander at what the other guys are doing. Of course, there are also online tools for this, but it's faster to just look at the competition. Then, take one of their leads, reduce it to a "keyword phrase" and paste it into your keyword search tool. This tells you what terms real people are putting into search engines. Because real people seldom type a whole, grammatically correct query into a search, their search strings tend to be jacked. "Live to 100," for example.

We wrote the headlines first. Then we ginned up a couple hundred words of pith whilst paying attention to "keyword density," which means we repeated the elements of the search term over and over in the verbiage of the piece. I used to write in English. This was making crossword puzzles for robots.

Despite the fact that the resulting pieces were barely longer than a personal ad, we break it up with a jump to another page. By doing this, we effectively double the amount of impressions the advertising injected all over the page will get, since it's paid for in units of a thousand impressions.

Adriane, the Editrix, routinely bitched how she had to Search-Engine-Optimize my copy before she clicked "publish." She also undid all of the Associated Press Style Manual ticks I had accrued over the years with much dedication and practice – if you're not printing the street number, don't abbreviate Boulevard to Blvd. It was about saving space and ink back in the day. Now, the notion is irrelevant. So, it seems, is everything I learned in J-school and by extension, me.

In short, I wasn't really writing. I was playing a kind of video game with words. And I sucked at video games. But we gave the people what they wanted. Hence, "How to Live to 100" – the keyword-centric headline assignment at hand. And since we were a hyper-local news portal, I had to inject some "local relevance" into it. "Lumaville Man's Longevity Secrets" would've sufficed but all I could think about was "Parallel Universe Experiment Sends Old Man, Boy to Shit hole – Failed Journalist Faces Quandary."

The Quandary? To pitch or not to pitch what could be the greatest story of my career to the Editrix? I could only imagine that she was growing as bored as me with our so-called editorial process. But what did I know? She wrote with her thumbs and spelled with numbers.

I found her at her desk, her eyes lost in the blue-glow of a tablet. She was writing, if you could call it that, but it looked more like she was playing a theremin as her hands wove through the air in some kind of editorial kabuki. Or maybe she had found a finger-painting app. The jury was out.

"How's the oldster?" she asked.

"Alive."

"And the centenarian?" she said.

"Well played," I muttered. I readied myself for some more degradation: "What if I told you I have a real story – one that could frontline us both for an award or two. You as editor, me as scribe."

"I'm listening," she said, then tugged her turquoise earbuds out to prove it.

"Government conspiracy, weird science, multigenerational victims, the end of the world as we know it..." I sang the last bit only to realize mid-phrase that

Adriane would never have heard the R.E.M. song.

She sighed: "The old dude died, didn't he?" She looked up, finally, and darted her almond-shaped eyes at me in a perfect pantomime of disgust. "Sit."

There wasn't a chair so I pulled one from a desk neighboring Adriane's. I hadn't seen Edwin, the lanky, bespectacled editorial assistant whose chair it was, until after I sat down. He glared at me. I stared back at him until he shook his head and walked away.

Adriane looked back down at her tablet, a churlish smile working the corners of her mouth. She liked my occasional alpha-dog moves, but only because she was still building an arsenal of her own. It would only be a matter of time before she would ward me off my own chair but I was pleased to be her mentor if only momentarily.

"Remember the shooting earlier? The fat guys?"

"Yeah, the release came in from the cops. You didn't tell me they were the TV commercial guys," she said. "I gave it to Edwin for the video blog."

Somehow that made sense, I guess.

"There was a kid who also witnessed the shooting. Later, when the cops had me in to cooperate, they had the kid there, but the deal was he didn't exist," I said.

"You lied?"

"No, I mean he didn't exist in any database," I said. "Detective Shane ran him upwards and sideways through every system they have and he was a non-entity."

"So, what? His parents lived off the grid. He was home-birthed and home-schooled," she said. "I was born in a kiddie pool in the living room and didn't have a real birth certificate until my fucking hippie parents sent me to public school."

"But he was wearing a private school jacket."

"People knick jackets all the time, don't they?" she said.

I reflexively covered the faded chalk X on my pocket as her eyes went back to her tablet. Check.

"It's possible the kid slipped through some rift in the space-time continuum. Just like the hundred year-old. They had the same story."

"They both saw the fat guys shoot each other? So, was everyone invited to this party except me?"

"No, no, they had matching stories about not belonging in this world, but..."

"If you're attempting some kind of disenfranchised youth-and-elderly angle, stop it. Our readers don't need to think. They don't even need to read. They just need to click-through all the shit we put on the trail of sensationalism." Checkmate.

I couldn't tell what appalled me more – Adriane's reductionist view of our gig or that she was right.

* * *

I popped in my earbuds and cued up my interview with Mac. Better me sifting for the quotes than having a dude halfway around the world doing a wholesale transcription. They get paid by the word, so every utterance, every "um" and "you know" and "uh, uh, uh" makes it into the text. It's faithful and annoying. Like a biblical literalist.

I cracked open my laptop. Since I'm a habitual procrastinator, I checked my email. I shouldn't have. There was another love letter from my secret admirer. Another fauxbituary. If I had any sense, I'd start collecting these little masterworks for publication. Or at least as evidence when they found my bloated corpse in the Lumaville river. I let my eyeballs bounce off the text for a second while hovering the mouse over "delete." That's when I realized that this fauxbit was different than its predecessors.

Dear Mr. Howell – I won't expect you to believe seeing as you're presently reading these words and probably feeling quite attuned to the fact that you're conscious enough to interpret their meaning. Maybe. Anyway, I want you to know, however, that you're not. You're a deadman, Mr. Howell. Dead. Like your career but more so. If that's even possible. If you care to see what's going to happen to you, read the attached description. You owe me at least that much...

I clicked on what appeared to be a Word file. Nothing happened so I decided to delete the email and pretend I'd never read it. I clicked "Delete." Nothing happened. I went to click it again and realized that my laptop had frozen. I did a hard restart. After a moment of grinding its way back to life the laptop froze again.

A pit grew in my stomach. I could hear my inner IT-guy chiding me for clicking on an attachment from someone who clearly wished me harm. I had unlocked a virus. And now my computer was dead. It was a work computer with nothing of consequence but the last couple months of my work on it, which was also nothing of consequence. Besides, I had my smartphone.

I opened my recording app. Mac's interview was alive and well. I could transcribe from the phone, which I nearly dropped when, on cue, it rang.

The pit in my stomach grew larger. I felt like an avocado – a huge pit and various shades of green. The number was blocked. It was either my future assassin or the Order of the Golden Star Credit Agency stalking a Mini Cooper payment. I answered. It was Shane.

"If you're inviting me to a ride along, I think I'll pass," I said.

"Well, that's too bad, Howell. I was even going to let you play with the walkie-talkie. So, Jude, the kid who knew your secret name, Rumpelstiltskin, or whatever..."

"I think I believe him."

"Wait. What?" Shane said. I had caught her off guard – first time.

"I believe, Jude's story."

"Cute. But doesn't do me a lick of good, Howell," she said, then added matter-of-factly, "because I don't know where he is."

"What do you mean?" I asked. "Parents pick him up? Caseworker? His attorney? I'll keep going until you say something..."

Shane blew a deep sigh then said "He escaped."

I laughed. When I realized my laughter wasn't being echoed I stopped. "He escaped? From you?"

"Not from me. But yes, he escaped. Tricked the admins with some of that mental jujitsu he's got in him. Went for a pee. Never came back."

Somehow, I wasn't surprised. The kid seemed canny. In fact, some part of me was impressed, but my admiration was cut short.

"Was wondering if you'd seen him on account of the fact that he seems to know so much about you," Shane said. I didn't like where this was going.

"The kid knows nothing about me," I said. Maybe too quickly. "I've never seen him before in my life. And you know that, Shane."

"All the same," she said, "You keep me posted. If you see even a kid that looks like him, you call me. Be in touch."

Panic is a sick little bitch that crawls up on your belly, warms it with her breath, then sinks a fang. My machine was kaput and the kid who allegedly traversed a universe to meet with my indifference had gone missing.

And I was on deadline.

I needed a drink. Actually, I needed 10 milligrams of Lorazepam, which I had in my pocket. But I needed the drink to wash them down. I already knew where I was going. And where I'd wake up...

9.
Dr(ink)

Unlike Mac's disappearing speakeasy, I knew my place was still there as it had always been, on the corner of Western Avenue and American Alley. It was far enough away from the U that the frat-boy factor was reduced to just future lifers and die-hards who were probably alcoholics before they arrived. The rest were neighborhood people. And Crysta the Barista.

She was lean, with skin made of bone china and hair drawn into a tight ponytail like a sable paint brush. You could see how she was still pretty if you had her yearbook photo as a point of reference. I only ever saw Crysta in a professional capacity, which meant "at night," so for all I knew she was a vampire, who liquored up her victims and awaited them in the alley after hours. The free pint Crysta pulled me suggested I might be next. But she wasn't a vampire. I'd woken up in her bed at least twice before and wasn't drained of anything more than a DNA sample and my self respect. And even if she was, she couldn't hurt me – I was a small town newspaperman. I was already undead.

The joint reeked like stale beer and the industrial-grade cleaning product that emanated from the restroom every time someone opened its door. The bar itself was dusted with the briny powder of peanut shells and was propped up by a raft of losers who kept the same half-dozen classic rock songs rotating on the jukebox. It's as if time had stopped in the place but no one knew precisely when.

I fished in my coat pocket for the little orange pill bottle. I had stripped the prescription sticker off the plastic cylinder because it was no one's business that I ate anti-anxiety meds like breath mints. And it let me see in an instant where I stood. One left.

Lorazepam and I had been doing a danse macabre for the better part of a decade. Through rigorous experimentation, I discovered that feeling "normal" amounted to maintaining a symbiotic balance of coffee, booze and psychotropic drugs at all times. Or, at least, that's what I thought "normal" felt like. I couldn't remember. Nor could I fathom staying straight long enough to find out.

I popped the top and rolled the lone pill onto the simulated woodgrain bar. The pill was scored across its diameter which I aligned with my eyetooth. Years of strategic use had worn the tooth into the perfect tool for halving pills. Ten milligrams snapped to a prudent five without protest. Half would do. The other half went back into the bottle and into my pocket. "Do not try this at home, kids," I muttered as I took a swig of beer to wash it down. I had ten minutes to think about my next move before I wouldn't care anymore.

Despite Editrix Adriane's admonitions, I knew what story I was going to write and it wasn't going to be a keyword-rich birthday card to Mac the Centenarian. I also knew that without a functioning laptop, I could draft the piece on my phone straight into the cloud and pick it up later on Crysta's wifi or at the library if she was on her period.

"See that guy over there?" Crysta said as she tossed her paintbrush hair in the direction of a lanky beardling leaning against the space where a pay phone once hung. Like the young man's face, the wall was pocked and looked like pressed particle board. "He says he's a writer. Do you know him?"

This made me tense. My arms felt like a pair of spring-loaded tin toys. I looked him over. He had all the hallmarks of a wannabe. The fedora was the first giveaway. I caught his eye and he showed off his well-practiced ability to raise a single eyebrow. Sonofabitch. It was Edwin the editorial assistant whose chair I'd stolen. I turned back to Crysta. "He bothering you?"

"Not anymore than anyone else. But he seemed interested in a way that seemed, 'extra special.'"

"'Special' as in 'short bus' or...?" I asked.

"More like, 'Is he a cop?'"

"A cop wouldn't look that square," I said. "His name is Edwin. He's an editorial assistant at the blog."

"Had to tell him I had a boyfriend," she said. "And you're him tonight."

Normally, such a move appealed to my native sense of chivalry though I was half afraid Crysta thought it might stick. More to the point, I could see from Edwin's smug smile that he thought he had something on me. Catalog someone's habits long enough and you can see how they stitched themselves together. And which thread to pull to take them apart.

Could Edwin tell I was going rogue? That I finally had a story worth writing?

I pulled out my phone. It was dead. No worries. Digital dharma had nothing on my blue-and-white Portage brand reporter's notebook. I slapped it on the bar, a "No. 200," Gregg-ruled, only half used. Long ago, I'd calibrated my handwriting such that a full-page was three-column inches on the nose. Not that column inches mattered anymore.

I started with the lede. No questions, no quotes, no dictionary definitions. Those were my rules. All I got down on paper was "Dewey." I took another sip and figured it would come to me. Like it always did on deadline.

But it didn't. No matter how gung-ho or drunk I felt, I was avoiding the obvious. There was a kid lost in Lumaville, the moral obligation to whom no amount of pills or booze or careerist self-delusion could strikethrough. The story and Jude were one and the same. Mac was right. I needed the kid. Moreover, he needed me, which made me feel bad for the both of us.

"You saving this," Edwin asked as he patted the stool next to mine.

"It's yours. There, we're even," I said. He pretended not to know what I was talking about. Or at least, that's how I took it when he raised his goddamn eyebrow again.

He dangled his long, attenuated fingers over my notebook as if casting a spell.

"Always on the clock, huh?"

I folded it shut and returned it to my left inside coat pocket with the same cinematic ceremony of uncocking a gun.

"I'm on deadline."

"What's that like?" He wafted smarm like Callery pears in bloom.

"Imagine the Sword of Damocles. It's hanging by a horse hair above your head. Now imagine you're a sword swallower. That's what it's like to be on deadline. Didn't you go to J school?"

"Marketing."

"Then why are you in editorial?"

"I'm on a fact-finding mission."

"You join the UN or just vacationing with Sean Penn?"

"Who's Sean Penn?" he asked. "I'm launching my own

start-up. Won't need hacks like you. Everything you do can be replicated with an algorithm."

My vision narrowed into a tunnel I tried to keep on his eyes but kept slipping to his attempt at a mustache. The Lorazepam and beer were fighting dirty. This usually wasn't a problem except the new microbrews on the menu were hopped up so much that the alcohol was double my normal dose. If you can take what they give you in the gut, they'll aim lower until they find something to render inoperable. I'd have to slow down lest I lose my bunk privileges.

"To the algorithm," I toasted. I extended my pint toward Edwin's but he didn't connect. Instead, he drained his last sip, rolled up his sleeves and put his elbows on the bar. On each of his pale forearms was tattooed a vintage fountain pen. By the look of them, they were fresh, still healing. This, I assumed, was how he earned calling himself a writer. There were cheaper, less painful, ways but unfortunately for Edwin they required actual writing. By a human.

Edwin put a fiver on the bar and drummed his nails on his empty pint glass. Crysta ignored him.

"You're girlfriend doesn't like me," he said.

"She's not my girlfriend," I replied, which told him more about me than I cared him to know. His smile was more bitter than sour grapes. "Anyway, I doubt an algorithm could do what I do the way I do it."

"You're right," he snorted into his glass and cocked the fedora a notch up his forehead. "It would be much more efficient, no errors and never over deadline."

"And what about original reporting?" I said. "How's your algorithm in the field?"

"It can source data that's way beyond the tripe in your little book."

"What little book?" I was having trouble getting the jumplines to match. I trained the dwindling pinhole of my consciousness between Edwin's eyes like a bindi.

"The one in your pocket." He knuckled where the chalk X had been on my breast pocket. The tin toy spring in my arm batted his hand away.

"Don't touch me, Edwin."

I stared in his general direction and he stared back while Crysta floated over with a full pint and swapped out his glass. She took the five and knocked twice on the bar. Edwin broke first, snickered and sipped from his pint.

"Jesus, Howell. For a moment there I thought you were going to kill me," Edwin said. "Then I remembered you only kill interns."

Edwin's pained yelp was only slightly louder than the blare of the incongruous platitudes of Tom Petty blasting from the jukebox, but drew attention nonetheless. The flesh of his forearm twisted in my grip until the scab tore from his new tattoo and tiny rivulets of blood ran over my fingers. His beer splashed to the floor, followed by the glass. It smashed into lethal shards as Edwin swung his other arm around but I caught it with my free hand and wrung the blood from that tattoo as well. We were both impressed with how it seemed to spurt from the nib of the illustrated pen but, alas, there was no ink in his veins.

Everything went black.

10.
Welcoming Committee

We called him 1K, which I suppose is reason enough to jump off the Golden Gate Bridge. The nickname wasn't meant to sound like a low-rent robot – it was a reference to the fact that I had done some bullshit math on a napkin and came up with the notion that nine-hundred and ninety–nine people had leapt to their deaths from the Golden Gate Bridge. The joke in the newsroom was that my mopey new intern would soon be number one thousand, hence "1K." It was the kind of collegiate ribbing, the kind of high-fructose gallows humor that made newsrooms the sick dog we all loved to pet.

Even though my guestimation of the magic number was unfounded, I thought the pitch had a solid human interest angle. Or a travel angle, since the number of suicides, even if inaccurate, still pointed to the bridge's dubious honor as the most popular location in the world to end one's life.

Incidentally, the second most popular place in the world to commit suicide is Aokigahara. It's a forest in Japan, also known as the Sea of Trees. It's beautiful (I've read) and even has signage that discourages killing oneself. I presume it's second on the list since it lacks the inherent utility of also

being a means by which one can kill oneself. If you forget
your implement of death it's not like forgetting a corkscrew
– unless it is – in which case you're better off, since the
notion of hara-kiri by church key is, in a word, galling. The
Golden Gate Bridge, however, is both a romantic landmark
and a lethal weapon.

The story was a lark. Obviously, this was long before
the invention of "trigger warnings." To extend the wonky
metaphor, in our newsroom at least, the "safety" was always
off. I don't apologize for this – it was the nature of how we
operated and always had. Until that slow, dusty day, I had
never misfired.

I remember the police scanner chirping at the
photographer's desk. Flash was on assignment so I cocked
an ear expecting the usual local hokey-pokey. The radio
croaked "10-29 Golden Gate Bridge." I was rusty on
my California Highway Patrol 10-code so I looked it up
online: "suicide attempt." Not my beat, I thought. Then
the dispatcher said, "The subject is wearing an undershirt,
handpainted, with '1K.'"

The drive was a hundred-mile-an-hour blur. I held my
breath the entire way. I parked my new Mini Cooper, still
running, at Vista Point and ran toward the throng of people
and police gathering around 1K, perched on the rail only a
third into the span. I sliced the fog with my press pass, held
high above my head until I spotted the first of many cops.
I elbowed my way to him.

"That's my intern!" I panted. The stoic office was having
nothing of it until 1K himself called out above the din of
traffic routed around the highway patrol cars that lined the
right lane.

"Dade?"

"Let me talk to him," I insisted and the officer acquiesced
and pushed me through to the front of the crowd, which

was bowed in a semicircle around 1K on the pedestrian path.

The salt wind and flop sweat matted his hair against his forehead. The palms of his hands were orange like those of people who eat too many carrots or yams. It was paint, from the bridge, wearing off where he gripped it with whitened knuckles. The homemade 1K T-shirt was too large for him and gaped at his lean neck.

"...Why do we do it?" he asked for the thousandth time.

I said it again and again regretted it. "Deadlines...?"

But louder sang that ghost, "What then?"

* * *

I awoke with a start. There was a pressure on my chest like a succubus had been sitting on me all night painting her toenails. If there wasn't a frozen knife lodged in my head, perhaps one would make it feel better. I suspected it was either too early or too late. I tried to reach the nightstand for my watch but I was clenched in some kind of post-coital yoga by Crysta. I tried to extricate myself from her entwined limbs but she was a Gordian Knot of arms, legs and biological imperative that would be impossible to escape without waking. Fortunately, someone else did it for me.

"Mom?" asked a freckle-faced young boy as he knocked on the door and it opened. He looked about ten and had a baseball cap pulled low on his forehead. Plumes of red hair curled around his ears. Crysta instantly snapped awake.

"You're not supposed to walk in here without knocking," she said sternly.

"I knocked," he said. He looked me over, then asked matter-of-factly, "Are you my dad?"

"Charlie!" Crysta yelped as her cheeks reddened with rage and embarrassment.

Charlie nodded, I think relieved. "Okay, I didn't think so." He closed the door.

Crysta was out of bed in a beat. She shook her paintbrush head, the ponytail of which had exploded into a tangle of spider legs. "I'm so sorry. He's going through a phase," she said.

"Goes straight for the hard-hitting questions," I said.

"Poor kid," she said. "The only person in the whole wide world he has is me. What luck, right?" She feigned a wry smile but she could tell I half agreed with her. I tried to cover it.

"It's not who you are but how you are," I said, impersonating a drugstore greeting card aisle. It sounded half right but came out all wrong. Crysta finished buttoning her shirt and studied me.

"Does it hurt?"

"What?"

"Your body."

I did a quick inventory. Yes, my body hurt but in new and exciting ways. Was this impact of 40 arriving all at once? There was something floating in my mouth. I feared it was a tooth, but it was just mouth crap.

"You passed out. On top of that weirdo."

"I what...?"

"You were doing some sort of two-handed arm wrestling thing with this guy, then, splat. You fell on top of him. Took three hipsters to pull you off. The dude was suffocating."

"Oh, that's all," I said. I tried to shrug but my shoulders ached as if I'd been carrying a railroad tie all night. Crysta bit her lip to conceal the smile curling on her lips. "But wait, there's more..."

"You came to for a bit while on top of him and listed every

film that had ever starred Sean Penn, for some reason," she said. "Then, I think, you kissed him."

"Sean Penn?"

"No, the dude. You were trying to make some sort of point. About method acting."

"How well did I make it?"

"Not well."

"Figures. I'm a writer, not an actor," I said as I rolled my feet to the floor. I was still wearing my Beatle boots but no pants.

"Uh-huh. Anyway, when I got you here, you insisted on eating frozen pot pie, still frozen... And then... And then we kind of did it. Kind of."

"Was I disgusting?"

"Tell you this much, Mr. Penn – you never broke character."

"Spicoli?"

"'I Am Sam.'"

In the motion picture version of my life, this is the point at which I would've thrown up. It didn't happen. That would come later. Instead, I swallowed hard and went to work assembling myself into an approximation of a man. If I wasn't back in action, at least I could get back in my action figure suit.

Crysta watched me dress with a kind of clinical reserve. Usually, our morning-after conversations were like talking to a pharmacist. "Did it work for you? Were there any complications? Good, okay, see you in about 30 days."

"I'll make some coffee," Crysta said. "Then you have to go. I have to think of something to tell Charlie."

"I didn't know you had..."

"You don't know a lot about me," she said as she straightened the bed. She clucked her tongue. "Dade..."

"Yep."

"We're not going to do this again, okay?" She attempted a frown. I nodded and did the same.

* * *

Charlie was eating a bowl of cereal and fiddling with his mom's smartphone. I straightened my coat and felt my own pressing phone against my aching ribs from my right inside pocket. I remembered I had to transcribe my interview with Mac.

Charlie looked up and then back at the phone. I hovered by the kitchen sink getting my bearings. I stood, awkward and silent. Finally, I asked, "What are you playing?"

"'The Knights of Skeldaria,'" he said as he dipped his freckle face toward the glowing rectangle against his palm. "It's a massive multiplayer online game. You team up to kill the Willogen."

"What's the Willogen?" I asked.

"I don't know, I haven't killed it yet. But this guy says he has. He's a legend."

Charlie swiped an orange thumb across the screen and gave the phone to me as he returned to his cereal. Frozen on the phone was a cartoonish avatar of a knight in shining armor under which was a gaming handle: a J, two zeroes and a D.

"How do you even pronounce that?"

Crysta cracked her bedroom door open far enough so that I could see she had changed her clothes for some reason. She dangled my car key from a bony finger. It was my cue to go.

"It's downstairs," she said. "You were in no condition."

I gave the phone back to Charlie, took my key and tried to exit through the broom closet.

* * *

Outside, the world was slick with dew, which made every car on the block look like it just had its paint touched up. Even the Mini. I ran my hand over the its roof and swept some cool beads of water over the edge where they streaked down the windshield and soaked into the parking ticket pinned beneath the wiper. I had stayed ten minutes too long. I knew this, but it was kind of the Lumaville Parking Enforcement to remind me.

As I drove down the boulevard, I took the opportunity to catalog my regrets. I kept a partial list tattooed on my soul, which I always revisited when hungover.

I probably would have been a damn fine teacher like my parents but resisted because real writers write, not teach, which I told them. I sired an abortion. I should have married Annika Strang but couldn't fathom being hitched to a woman who spelled her name like that. In second grade, I let a mentally disabled kid miss the bus when I could have stopped it. I pursued a reckless story that contributed to my intern's suicide.

The apartment I used to share with my ex was directly above Cafe Purgatorio on Western Avenue. Which is to say I have a built-in alarm clock thanks to the baristas below who bang their portafilters like a judge's gavel. This begins at 6 a.m. and ends about sixteen hours later. In the coffee court everyone is out of order.

The building was stately if smallish. Probably built in the 1930s with just enough ornate architectural features to suggest someone cared back when there was hope for the neighborhood. The area was fairly well gentrified at this point. The sidewalks were crowded with strollers and dogs and a steady stream of "knowledge workers" flowing into the cafes, florists, eateries and organic grocers. It was cheaper than San Francisco but not by much. Just enough to keep it vaguely arty. I suppose that's what a knowledge worker is – a wannabe artist with a decent day job and a well curated stream of Twitter twaddle to justify their hip eyewear.

There was space to park around the corner on Fourth, which meant an H-bomb had gone off and wiped out my neighborhood (yes!) or it was street cleaning day. I went with the H-bomb option and parked. My neighbor, a round fellow with a full beard and Greek fisherman's cap was fidgeting at the bottom story door. I hadn't bothered to learn his name in the two years I lived down the hall from him. I was beginning to fret I'd have to make some small talk as he attempted yet another key in the lock. He finally found the one he was looking for and trundled his steaming takeout boxes upstairs. The stink of fried octopus, grease and fish filled the hall and would persist, I surmised, until the next morning as it always did. The man made a wary nod toward me just before his door clicked shut, followed by the snaps and clacks of about half a dozen deadbolts, door chains and other hardware. He lived in the building before the neighborhood had improved, but it always seemed his security ritual was a critique of me personally.

I reached my key to my lock but didn't need to turn it. The door was already a half inch ajar. Fucking cleaning people, I thought. Then I remembered I fired the cleaning service. I told them it was because they threw away some notes I'd made on a cocktail napkin, which I had convinced myself contained the greatest idea ever written. But it was really because...

A figure passed by the slim view of the door jam.

Butterflies erupted in my stomach. I took a step back and held my breath. I did an inventory of everything of value I had in the place. The grand total was nothing – my laptop was toast and my phone was in my pocket. Everything else was clothes, books and dirty dishes. Or more accurately, dirty clothes, dirty books and clean dishes. I never ate at home.

I reached into my coat pocket for my pen. The closest implement I had to a weapon. I clicked it so the tip popped up, like a switchblade. It was pathetic but there was a chance the other guy might have to bother with a cap so I'd have the jump. That's assuming the intruder was another writer. Given the finesse with which my fauxbituaries were written this tracked. The pen is mightier than the sword and "sword" is just "words" spelled by a dyslexic.

I kicked the door open, like in the movies. It flew wide, hit the wall and ricocheted shut. Shit. But at least in the half second it was open, I not only saw the culprit, I stunned him. He was shorter than I expected and I didn't figure he would cry.

Jude stood in the middle of what passed as my living room. He wiped the tears from his eyes with one hand while holding a framed photo he'd plucked from the piano in the other.

"You have terrible instincts for a thief," I said once I started breathing again, which was a minute longer than either I or Jude anticipated.

"There's a wall safe behind the Matisse print," I said and gestured to the large, tattered *Icarus, From Jazz* that claimed most of the kitchen wall as its own.

Time had faded the cheap print so that the once-blazing orange-red heart in Ike's black chest was now grey.

"The combination is my birthday. And I probably don't need to tell you what that is, seeing as you already know too much about me to be playing straight anyway."

Jude put the photo back on the piano. He then adjusted it with improbable care.

"You know her?" I asked with a nod to the photo. It was my ex. Annika Strang – Annie – all dark tresses and ice blue eyes.

"Do you?" Jude asked with a kind of defensive impertinence kids can do when pubescent.

"How did you get in?"

He fished a key from his pocket and put it on the piano.

"Hide-a-key," he said. "I remembered where to look."

"You've been here before? What, are you some kind of stalker too?"

He looked shocked. Offended even. He steeled himself.

"No," said Jude. "Guys like you are just predictable. And the fake rock the key was hidden inside stood out like a Christmas ornament. Not that you would know what that is anyway."

I looked around the room. The kid had nested on the couch. It looked like he'd spent the night. My newish duvet cover was bunched into a ball in the corner. A couple of cereal bits floated in a half bowl of milk on the coffee table – next to the empty beer can peeking from a brown paper bag. I snatched the can from the table and attempted to crush it in front of the boy's face. It kind of folded a bit but sufficiently underscored my accusation.

"So, you broke into my apartment, drank my booze and slept it off on my couch?"

Jude shook his head, more in pity than denial and said,

"No, man. That's your beer can – one of the 30 or so left all over this dump and I didn't break in. I used the key, which you left outside in a fake rock that might as well have a sign on it that says, 'Come on in, beer inside.' And cereal. I did eat your cereal. At least I think it was cereal. It was petrified, whatever it was."

"Sorry the accommodations are not to your liking, kid, but fortunately I'm not running a foster home," I said as I whipped out my phone. I scrolled to Detective Shane's contact info and flashed her mugshot at the kid to give him a preview of who he'd be slumming with next.

"Remember her? She's looking for you."

His eyes widened and he balled his fists.

"Don't! Please don't call the cops!" he pleaded.

"Why? You're a runaway, in my house, eating my petrified cereal."

"Because I'm in trouble."

"No shit, you're in trouble."

"I need your help. To get back. Before... Before they get me," Jude panted. His breath had grown shallow and staccato. He was beginning to hyperventilate. Or was method acting – the jury was still out.

I put my hand on his narrow shoulder and leaned him back on the couch. I grabbed the beer can bag and put it up to his mouth.

"Breathe," I said. "Or you'll pass out."

Jude did his best to slow his breath but it wasn't until his brown eyes connected with mine that he began to calm down. Then he broke his gaze, awkward, maybe embarrassed. That's when I decided to believe him. He could feign all manner of emotions with his elastic, preadolescent face but his eyes couldn't lie. At least he hadn't learned that trick yet. He took a deep breath and slumped into the couch. What he didn't know is that I already believed him. But I wasn't going to let him know that.

"I get anxious sometimes," he said, defeated.

"It's okay," I said. "So do I. Now, we're going to take this real slow," I began as I rose from the couch.

"I'm going to make some coffee, which should give you

just enough time to get your story together. And it better be a good one."

He nodded. I walked into the kitchen and opened the freezer where I kept the grounds from Cafe Purgatorio.

"And if there isn't any milk left for my coffee, I'm going to be really pissed," I teased from behind the door.

Under his breath, I could hear him say, "You don't take milk in your coffee."

He was right. And then I threw up.

11.
The Knights of Skeldaria

The Swedish government subsidizes the installation of garbage disposals for apartment building sinks to encourage the production of bio-gases, which they collect for energy. For some reason, Annika's repatriated Swede parents received two and decided to send one to us. All the way from Sweden. The shipping alone cost more than an American disposal. But there it was, our Swedish garbage disposal. We bragged that we had the only "true" Ikea kitchen in the building. We put everything down the hole: The vile mushroom from her homemade kombucha, pencil shavings, all manner of pasta, coffee grounds, part of a spoon, residue from every recipe in the Laurel's Kitchen cookbook. After all, it was a Volvo, not a Chevy. We were awesome then, we had a European garbage disposal, installed by an out-of-work aerospace engineer I found on Craigslist. We were living large – I was at the paper, she was wrapping a thesis on artificial intelligence or something.

But as I vomited the last of the previous night's swill into the sink, I noticed for the first time the brand name molded into the disposal's rubber splash guard. "InSinkErator" – an American brand, in fact, the American brand. The disposal wasn't Swedish, it just made the round trip from a European vacation and faked a Swede accent for kicks. Now all the truth is out, I thought, as I flipped the disposal's switch. It ate the puke with aplomb. God bless America.

The disposal finished in a final turgid belch, Jude shook his head and said "Gross."

He was sitting on my couch – the only piece of furniture she left behind. It was also the one I truly did not want. It was like a 400 pound "fuck you" that served to remind me A) of her; and B) that I didn't have any friends willing to help me move it. Now it was the bed of an alleged quantum fugitive. I needed coffee before my mind broke.

"Who is she?" Jude asked. He pointed to the photo of Annika.

"You sure know how to zero in on a sore spot. That's my ex. Why? Do you know her real name too? Do share so I can forward her mail."

He just stared at the photo with a quizzical expression.

"She looks so young," he said. "And pretty."

"Still is. I bet. But that was then." I said, looking over his shoulder. I tossed the duvet on the couch. "This is now. Big difference so far."

"Like how?"

"I've gotten used to not having a roommate."

Jude got up and moved the photo so that he could see it from the couch, then plopped down again and asked, "Where were you last night?"

"Precisely," I said. "I've grown accustomed to being unaccountable. What's your angle?"

"She makes me feel like everything is going to be fine," he said, staring at the photo, which was really just a pixelated blowup of an image I pulled from Facebook after the fact.

But I knew what he meant. Annie always conveyed hyper-competence in the set of her jaw and the way she shaped her brows. Petite people knew how to do that. They spend half their lives proving they're capable, then coast on the pervading foreknowledge of their ability to manage. I was still using her method to make coffee – a melon baller. I scooped four perfectly rounded tablespoons of coffee grounds into the French press and turned on the kettle.

It had been just enough time that the shit that bugged me about her began to fade and only the longing and regret remained. Twenty-twenty hindsight meets rose-tinted glasses.

After a moment, the kettle began to steam. I caught it before it whistled since this particular kettle blew an off note. I purchased it at the Le Creuset outlet on the cheap. It had no outward damage, just the sad secret that it couldn't sing like a regular kettle. Annie left that behind too.

I poured the water over the grounds and stirred them with a wooden spoon (never metal) and waited for the bloom. After a beat, the liquid went from deep black to a creamy brown, like the coat of a newborn foal. I set the timer on my phone to precisely four minutes. If the coffee brewed any longer it would turn bitter.

I had three and half minutes to shake down the kid before pressing the plunger down on the coffee. I watched the grounds dance and twirl in the midnight of the French press. Or "Le Figaro" as Annie called it, after the newspaper in France.

"So, now that I've committed a felony on your behalf, I'd like to get some clarity on a couple of issues," I said.

"I'm game, what issues you got? Besides the obvious," he said with just enough hustle that it occurred to me I might have wandered further into his con.

"The first issue that has ensnared my enfeebled mind," I said, planting the seeds of my defense, "How did you know my original name?"

"Kit Fergus?" he said, turning to me. "Because that's your

name. At least, that's how I've always known you. But not like this."

"What do you mean 'not like this?' You mean in your version of reality?"

"For starters, you're thinner in my version."

He looked at me with a blank expression then got up and paced the room. He stepped toward me as tears began to well in his eyes and went in for a hug. I let him hang for a moment, then I remembered how impossible it was to accept, let alone, ask for a hug when I was his age.

I patted him on the back as he began to sob. I looked at my phone over his shoulder. The coffee was going to be bitter.

"Hey, there little, man, we'll work this out," I attempted to soothe, at a loss.

"I'm scared. I didn't mean to do this. I know I shouldn't have done it."

Now, we were getting somewhere. "What did you do?"

He broke free and returned to the couch where he crumpled into a ball.

"I took something that I wasn't supposed to."

"What was it?"

"You're not going to turn me in, right?"

"We're in this together now. But you owe me the whole story," I said. "What are you hiding?"

"Nothing," he retorted, as if I had accused him.

"Listen," I said, "I've done enough interviews to know when someone is lying to me."

He started to spill – just the facts, ma'am. I'd find the truth later.

It came down to homework. He hadn't completed his lesson on classical mythology, and he received a negative progress report that necessitated a parent's signature. Upon presenting the report to his mother (his father apparently was out of the picture), he was promptly scolded and punished by having his phone privileges revoked. Specifically, his mobile phone privileges. A preteen mobile phone? Yep, he was one of those. His mother never wanted him to have the phone in the first place, but his absentee father had given him the late model iPhone so that he may have a point of access to him, or vice-versa. It was patently obvious to all concerned the phone was a consolation prize for the kid's having struck out in the paternity lottery.

The phone wasn't the issue so much as app on it. A game – *The Knights of Skeldaria*, the same sword and sorcerer saga baking the brains of Crysta's kid. One had to defeat the fearsome Willogen with something called the "Pentacle Charm." Jude said he'd done it before and it unlocked an Easter Egg in the game. He didn't elaborate and I was already two leagues out of my depth so I didn't ask. Given my permanent protest against popular culture, this is all I needed to know – thanks to the gloss in archetypes courtesy of Lumaville State – The Knights win. At least they should.

Jude went to school phoneless, which made his show-and-tell no show and all tell, thus deepening the crevice of humiliation that was forming a chasm that threatened to reach the core of his being. The next stop would surely be a black trenchcoat.

On the train home, while the other prepubescent hoodlums huddled in the back of the car with their digital devices chirping away as they attempted networked triumph over the Willogen, Jude felt even more lacking.

This is when he spotted the woman vigorously rummaging her pockets a few seats down. Jude thought at first she had misplaced her ticket – an easily remedied issue that he himself had experienced on a couple of occasions. If you're disinclined to jump the turnstile, you can always cough up some crocodile tears and the station manager will usher you through the handicap door. However, when the train stopped at the north end of the Boulevard, the woman bolted up, patting her coat pockets as if each were emitting a small flame. Then she started out the door. What he was looking for, Jude realized, was what she had been sitting on. An iPhone – not unlike the one Jude had forfeited earlier on account of his disinterest in Theseus' slaying of the Minotaur.

Jude scurried over to the woman's former seat and sat upon the phone like a mother hen atop an egg. The doors of the train closed. A beat later, it vibrated on his butt and he nearly leaped to the ceiling. This gave him momentary vantage to the woman at a payphone. Jude deduced that it was the woman calling herself to locate the missing phone. It didn't take much to arrive at this conclusion given the pang of guilt that flashed in his tummy when his eyes met those of the woman's just as the train rolled away.

Interesting? Perhaps. But the headline, "Kid Steals Phone" wasn't going to win me the Blogger of the Year Award. But that wasn't the nut.

"She had the game," Jude said. "On her phone."

"The game?"

"'The Knights of Skeldaria,'" he said. "I hit it and logged in. That's when everything changed."

I leaned back and and looked down at my hands. Unconsciously, I had scribbled several pages of notes in my reporter's notebook. Still got it, I thought, never crossed my mind to record an interview. I reached into my pocket for my phone. I looked at it a second, then had an inspiration:

"Show me," I said. I tossed Jude the phone. "Download 'The Knights of Skeldaria' and show me."

12.
We Can Be Heroes

Jude was up for the challenge.

"Old phone. It probably can't handle it," he said. "You should get a new phone."

"You're stalling," I said. "Download the Knights of Whatever..."

"Skeldaria," he said with a sigh and proceeded to poke at my phone. "What's your password?"

I hesitated just long enough for him to say "Nevermind" and hack into my apps account.

"You sure?" he said, eyebrows raised. "If it turns into a brick it's between you and Steve Jobs – not me, okay?" He keyed and swiped like a pro. He gave the phone back to me with a sigh meant to emphasize his self-exoneration. I looked at the phone. Nothing appeared to be happening.

"It's downloading," he said and shook his head. "It's going to take a while. Old phone."

"We can wait," I said. I glanced at the "estimated download time" and exclaimed, "Three days?"

"Like I said."

"What are you downloading – all of Wikileaks?"

"'The Knights of Skeldaria' is a massively multiplayer role-playing game. It's big. Your phone is old and the

Internet connection is shit."

"It's not my Internet connection," I said. "It's the cafe's downstairs. Works better by the window."

Jude sighed.

I raised the sash of one of the street side windows and sat on the sill. Outside, a streetcleaner chugged up the block inhaling leaves. Its orange beacon light reflected off the surrounding apartment windows.

The phone screen flashed to life. On it was a graphic of a hairy squid-like creature surrounded by armored knights, accompanied by heraldic fanfare in tinny, eight-bit audio. A login prompt popped up. "It wants a password," I said.

Jude's cheeks were flushed.

"Are you sure," he asked. I nodded. "Make one up."

I put in my usual and as usual I reminded myself to change it someday.

The phone went black again.

"Now what?"

Jude's eyes were closed and his hands were over his ears. After a moment he winked an eye open, then composed himself. He cleared his throat.

"You should be logged in now."

"It's just black," I said. "The knights, the hairy thing, gone."

"That's the Willogen."

"Well, it's gone," I showed the phone to Jude who just shook his head.

"Because your phone is now a brick," he said. I could tell he was relieved.

"What do you mean?"

"You killed it."

"What do you mean I killed it?" A fireball of heartburn lit in my chest.

"Your phone couldn't handle the data surge and it died.

You killed it. Call Steve Jobs."

"Steve Jobs is dead."

"What? Really?" Jude said. He was legitimately astonished. "This place sucks. That's like the worst thing ever."

But it wasn't. Not to me. The worst thing ever was that my phone was dead and my interview with Mac the Centenarian was in it. And I was past deadline.

* * *

For Jude's sake I tried my damnedest to remember what it was like to be a kid on the cusp of his teens. When I was his age, *Return of the Jedi* was just hitting theaters. My mother used to buy tickets to the big screen cinemaplex which showed 70 millimeter prints of all the *Star Wars* films and I remembered how punk I felt wearing a *Revenge of the Jedi* T-shirt to the opening. I remembered baking my bare feet on the hot asphalt between the community pool and the ice cream truck, when four sweaty quarters could buy a Missile Pop or a Fudgesicle peddled by a reformed carnie with a Class B driver's license. I remembered older girls who smelled like piña coladas, who talked endless shit and I was mesmerized by the suburban exotica of their oversized concert shirts worn like caftans atop neon bikinis. I remembered afternoons lost to an nth generation VHS tape of *Risky Business* freeze-framed on Rebecca De Mornay's naked breasts. And here, Jude and his ilk could call up a panoply of porn on a handheld device with such ease that it probably bored them. I was old. Old enough, in fact, to be Jude's father and suddenly very glad I wasn't. For his sake. What I did I know about anything? Mine was the last generation of innocence.

I splashed some water on my face, brushed my teeth, contemplated shaving and decided to change my shirt instead. I went into my closet and perused what was left of the week's action figure outfits. Not much. I pulled the T-shirt off my back, threw on its twin and pulled a button-down off the hanger.

Piano music caught my ear from the living room. The Marche Funèbre. It was too good for a kid and went to investigate and make sure Chopin hadn't also found the hide-a-key.

Jude was behind the keys, absorbed in the music he was making. This, at least, was an endorsement for piano lessons – self-soothing. If I'd have stuck with it perhaps there'd be more piano and less pinot in my life.

The kid looked up, did a couple trills while our eyes locked.

"For Steve," he said as he squinted at me.

Then he started laughing.

"You always wear a Superman shirt under your clothes?" He didn't miss a note.

I looked at the ensemble I was still buttoning and sure enough, I was wearing a Superman t-shirt underneath the button down.

"Hey, some people wear crosses, Stars of David, I wear a Superman shirt. He's the patron saint of reporters. You know, because of Clark Kent."

"I used to have Superman underwear too," says the kid. "But then, you know, I turned 10."

I looked at him awhile, long enough for him to squeeze an apology in before I said it was time to go. There was work to do. I had to get back to the old folk's home and redo my interview with Mac. Looked like I was going to have a sidekick.

I reached for the hall light switch and missed. Years ago,

the ex and I lived next door in the adjoining apartment, the layout of which, down to the fixtures and switches, was a mirror of this apartment. I've never gotten used to it and am constantly reaching for phantom light switches from muscle memory.

"Other side," said Jude.

And we left, in this new constellation, a pair of dishevelled wandering stars.

* * *

Back on Western Avenue the streets were clean, except around the Mini where tawny, orange and yellow leaves piled around it. A ticket on the windshield officially recognized my small contribution to the autumnal palette of Lumaville.

Jude buckled himself into the passenger seat and I gave him his first J-school tutorial.

"Okay, we're going on a gig. We're going to interview a hundred-year-old guy who might be able to help you."

"How's a hundred-year-old guy going to help me?" he said. "Am I in his will?"

"He's had a similar experience to yours. Right time, wrong place. But here's the deal – I'm the reporter. I'm Clark Kent. You're the sidekick, so you're Jimmy Olsen," I said. "You know who Jimmy Olsen is, right?"

"Is he an eighth-grader?"

"Uh, no. He was Clark Kent's photographer sidekick," I said. "You do know who Clark Kent is, right?"

"Yeah. Spoiler alert, he's Superman," Jude snorted.

"Thanks. Anyway, I need you to be the Jimmy Olsen to my Clark Kent for this assignment."

"Why do you get to be Superman?"

"Because I'm Clark Kent, the reporter," I said. "And I'm wearing the shirt."

"Can I be Spider-Man? Peter Parker is a photographer too."

"Fair enough – Parker," I said. "That phone of yours have a camera?"

"I think so," said Jude as he inspected the device. "You know that Superman is a DC and Spidey is a Marvel, right?"

"I have no idea what that means and I don't care."

"They would never meet in real life," he said. "Different universes."

"Like you and me," I said with a smile. Jude didn't reciprocate.

"Except for a couple of non-canonical inter-company collaborations, Superman and Spidey never met," he said. "Also, I know who Jimmy Olsen is. I was just being ironic."

"Uh-huh," I sighed. "Okay, here's the drill, we're going to an old people's home, so just be quiet and cute. And quiet. Mostly quiet."

I hooked a left on 5th and again on B. Jude pulled down the visor on his head and opened the mirror.

"I need a toothbrush," he said.

"Don't smile."

"No, seriously, I need to brush my teeth."

I pulled over and looked at him hard. He smiled. I couldn't begrudge the kid his hygiene.

"There's a drug store over there. Run in and get a tooth brush. And toothpaste too," I said, then added, "Hurry! Time is not on our side."

Jude unbuckled and squeezed past the car door. Then he stopped and opened it back up. He just looked at me.

"What?" I asked.

"I need money."

I sifted the dollar bills from the receipts in my coat pocket and handed him the wad. He scurried out.

That's when I noticed the phone. Jude's phone, the stolen phone – on the seat. I grabbed it and gave it a lookover. Nothing special about it – typical smartphone. A bit beefier than some, smaller than others. It did feel hotter than it should but that could because the kid was sitting on it. On the back was a sticker of a squid-like creature, blocky, as if it were rendered as an old school eight-bit computer graphic.

I thumbed through the apps on it. The usual suspects: map, browser, music, calendar, no games so far as I could tell, except maybe something with a sort of peculiar icon. It was the same image as the squid on the sticker. My thumb hovered over the icon but before I could activate it, the passenger door flung open.

"Don't do that," spat Jude with the brush still in his mouth. He looked like a mad dog, the toothpaste foaming in his mouth. "That's 'The Knights of Skeldaria,'" he spat. I gave the phone back.

"You got a recording app on that?"

"Yes."

"Camera?"

"Duh."

"Okay, you're in charge of it. Just do what I say."

He asked if I had any water. I fished around the back seat and produced an aluminum water bottle with some yoga studio logo on it. Another one of Annie's castoffs. As Jude rinsed and spit into the gutter, I couldn't remember when I had filled the bottle last and dreaded for a moment that Annie was the last to fill it – years ago. He didn't say anything about it tasting badly, so I didn't say anything about how it might. Kids are impressionable that way.

We took a right on Hayes and Jude looked to me for a

second, pale and weird.

"What?" I asked. "Is it the water?"

"Um, no, why?

"Nothing."

"I was just going to ask, who's Bizzaro's sidekick?"

"He doesn't have one."

"If you're Clark Kent, that means you think you're Superman. I think you're actually Bizzaro," Jude said matter-of-factly.

"Thanks, kid," I said, then corrected my grammar. "I mean, Bizzaro me thanks."

"So, what does that make me?" he asked.

"Bizzaro's sidekick, I guess."

"I was afraid of that."

I pulled to the curb across from a bus a shelter where half a dozen oldsters were lining up, donned in robes and clutching improvised luggage of plastic grocery store bags. After a moment a nondescript commuter van pulled up and they filed in. The van then pulled into the circular driveway of the Chaparral House and let them out. Neither Jude or I could make sense of the short ride. Instead, I told him to get the phone ready to capture the interview.

I'd need real recorded quotes to make this all work out. To make it believable, not just to the Editrix but to myself. The panic of being played came back but I batted it back figuring if the story didn't track, I could always fly some email interviews to neurologists, get a handle on this whole Capgras Syndrome phenomenon and with any luck pull a "disease of the week" angle out of it. And drop the kid off at the police station on the way.

At the reception desk, the same admin lady was cutting snowflakes in crepe paper. She must have been the only person trusted with scissors in the place. She didn't look up from her handiwork but greeted us just the same.

"You're back," she said. She glanced up at Jude and smiled. "And is this your assistant?"

"He's my photographer, actually," I said with that smirk that wins instant complicity when kids are around.

Jude produced his phone and took the lady's picture to sell the moment.

"Why, you're so handsome someone should be taking a picture of you," she said. "You look just like your dad."

"He's not my kid," I added needlessly, which slightly embarrassed the old lady. "Oh, well, you're lucky to have him working for you." The lady pointed down the hall with her scissors. "You remember where to go?"

I nodded and Jude and I made our way to room 209. On each door along the way were the plastic green medallions. Each read "I'm OK." This time they reminded me of that self-help book *I'm OK, You're OK*, which for a while, was like scripture with our parents. Whenever I saw the title, I couldn't help but snort, recalling a stoner pal in college who insisted the title was *Imok, You're OK* and would talk at length about Imok, who he imagined to be an affable Quasimodo-type. Shit gets weird when you're high.

"Why's everyone 'OK?'" asked Jude.

"It's how they tell the staff they're still alive."

"Grim," observed Jude.

There was no "I'm OK" sign on room 209. I knocked on the door and waited. I knocked again. Jude looked up at me and shrugged.

"Maybe he's not okay."

I knocked again. Nothing. I cleared my throat and knocked a little harder. Still nothing. I took a deep breath and shook my head.

"Hey, man, I'm sorry you had to see this. I didn't mean for you to..."

"How's he going to help me if he's not answering the

door?"

"Dude, I think you're missing the point. He's not answering the door because..."

I looked at Jude and leaned a little forward. It took a beat but he got it.

"Oh, shit," he said.

"Yep. You go tell that lady at the front desk. I'm going to see if I can get inside," I said.

"That sounds a lot more interesting," said Jude. "I'll go with."

"No you won't, you macabre little shit. Go tell the lady." Jude reluctantly started down the hall.

"Wait," I said. Jude brightened. "Give me the phone."

He slapped it into my palm and ran down the hall. I put it in my pocket. As soon as Jude turned the corner I turned the door knob. The door was unlocked.

Inside, it looked like business as usual, at least for a 100 year-old. Bottles of pills were everywhere. The hatbox of ancient newspaper clips was still out. So was Mac, sitting in his easy chair. His eyes were open – milky blue and staring forward into the void. He was wearing a suit and his wiry arms laid across his lap, one sleeve rolled to the elbow.

"Mac?" I asked. It was a perfunctory gesture. I could tell from his stillness that he was dead. In the light from his window I could see dust particles eddying around him like snowflakes, undisturbed by breath.

Then I remembered a stray science factoid about 90 percent of household dust being dead skin cells and realized I was watching decomposition in real time. Or it was just dust. I took a picture of Mac, aping the forensic shit I'd seen on TV. I was improvising, doing anything to make the moment productive, to allay the fact I no longer had a story. And Jude no longer had a character witness.

I had a dark thought. I knelt over the hatbox and begin

sifting the old papers until I found the famed "Dewey Wins" broadsheet. I carefully folded it under my arm. Mac would have wanted it that way – a gift from one reporter to another, I said to myself, but who was I kidding? I was a grave robber. The only thing Mac really wanted for me was to help the kid. His words echoed in my ears: "That's your story."

I shuffled over to Mac's galley kitchen and opened a couple of cupboards until I found the booze. My hands were shaking. Nerves – Mac's death and the impending doom of my blogging career were making me jangly. I poured a finger of semi-decent whiskey into a tumbler, raised the glass to Mac and put it back.

Or tried to – Jude's phone rang right as I tried to swallow and I ended up spraying a mouthful over Mac's corpse.

I patted him down with my sleeve trying not to disturb the body. The phone rang again. I reached for it in my pocket as I wiped Mac's dead face with the inside lining of my coat like a giant bird wing.

The caller ID was blocked. I answered it.

"Hello?"

"Who is this?" came the voice – accusatory, raspy.

"And who is this?" I parried.

I wished I hadn't asked.

13.

Needle in a Haymaker

I cleared my throat.

"Who is this?" I repeated.

The voice came cooly from the phone and chilled my ear.

"I'm the person whose stolen phone you're holding."

Check. But not quite checkmate.

"Maybe you dialed the wrong number."

"I think I know my own number."

I realized the voice wasn't male or female but treated by some kind of digital chicanery to sound genderless, robotic.

"What is it?"

"Why should I tell you?" the voice asked.

"To prove it's your phone."

"I could do that," said the voice. "Or I could just call the police."

"You're doing a lot of calling for someone who's missing her phone."

Despite the filtering, I detected an accent. Or was it an affectation? There was something overly mannered in the voice, as if its owner spent years in the theater or had learned English from watching Britty imports on public broadcasting.

"How 'bout you just stay put and I'll come down and get it?" they offered. I heard the plaintive pinging of an opening car door signal and a slam. They were already on their way. But where?

"Still at the Chaparral House?" the voice said.

And mate. They had me. Somehow the voice on the other end knew where I was and if they knew where I was they knew where Jude was. This didn't bode well for either of us.

I went to the window and parted the blinds with my thumb and forefinger. Nothing but a courtyard and oldsters ashing ill-begotten cigarettes in the fountain.

"You live here or something?" I said with a snort, buying time until could figure my next move.

"No one lives at a place like that," the voice laughed. "It's where you go to die."

I instinctively jerked around to see Mac, still as a mannequin in his chair. The room was beginning to spin a little. I held the phone out at arm's length, pinching like one would a snake. I hit the speakerphone icon and put the phone on the armrest of Mac's chair.

"Very sad, what happened to Mac," the voice continued, tinny from the phone's crappy speaker.

I knelt next to Mac's chair and looked at his bare forearm. It had caught my eye earlier and then realized now that my unconscious was trying to tell me something. The arm was bony and mottled with liver spots and patches of coarse hair.

"You mean very sad dying on his birthday?" I said.

"Well, yes, there's that, but surely he told you his story?" the voice said. "The facts of his case must've been interesting to you."

"I don't deal in facts. Just truth," I said. I'd been waiting weeks to say that.

"I see. Wait – am I on speakerphone?"

The voice sighed, then said in a slow and even tone: "You don't know the power you're messing with. I can help you. And the kid. He doesn't belong in your world."

"A lot of things don't belong in our world. David Bowie, for example, but he gets along just fine," I said. I tried to laugh.

The voice didn't like that. It became heated, shrill. It cracked like an arc welder: "Mess with me and I will... Fucking. End. You."

Then I saw it on Mac's arm – one tiny droplet of blood that looked as if it had bubbled to the surface after the slightest of pinpricks.

The fireplug nurse from the day before opened the door. She looked at me with kind eyes as she approached Mac, shaking her head. Two brawny orderlies followed, trailed by Jude. I reached for the phone, but the call was dead.

* * *

When a patient dies, whether at a hospital or a convalescent home, there's a procedure that's always followed. The employees are mandated by state law to examine each "decedent" for a probable cause of death before they move the body. As one can imagine, things get pretty lax around the old persons' home seeing as the most probable cause of death is being an old person. Consequently, the staffers barely take a pulse before wheeling out the old tenant and freshening the linens for the new one.

After checking a handful of boxes on her clipboard, the fireplug gave the nod and the gorillas in white scrubs lifted Mac by the ankles and armpits onto a gurney. They didn't show the slightest hint of strain as Mac's corpse bowed like an empty hammock.

"Did you check his pulse?" I asked impatiently.

The guy, who might have been a pro-wrestler in his youth, looked at me and said, "He's dead, man."

"Sure, I get that but did you check his pulse, or his heart or any of the shit you're supposed to do to make sure he's dead."

"Brother, I know this can be hard but the man is definitely dead."

"I know he's dead. Did you confirm why he's dead?"

"He was a hundred years old. That's why," said the orderly.

His buddy chimed in: "We all got a time. Hell, most the guys in my neighborhood didn't make it to thirty. This old dude did that three times and change. Just think of the shit he saw." The guy apologized for his language and nodded at Jude. The nurse took this as her cue to escort him out.

"Come on, handsome," she said as she ushered Jude out of the room with a hand that looked like pink crepe paper against his dark school jacket. "I gotta key to the vending machines," she said over her shoulder as they exited.

The first orderly slipped an army-green body bag over Mac's running shoes as the other turned the body on its side so the bag could be pulled beneath him.

"You're not going to take his shoes off?" I asked.

The second orderly looked over his shoulder, then leaned toward me. He whispered, "You want them?"

I pinched the bridge of my nose as I shook my head, then pointed to Mac's arm.

"Did you happen to notice the droplet of blood on his arm?"

The two lugs simultaneously grabbed an arm very nearly making Mac high-five himself. I persisted: "Look at his left arm. It looks like a pinprick. Like a needle. Was he a diabetic or something?"

"Not that we're aware of. He was in perfect health," said

the orderly.

"Then why did he die?"

"Because he was ancient, man. You just gotta accept that old people die, alright?"

The other orderly spotted the blood drop, which had crusted into a tiny scab.

"Yeah, here it is. Bug bite."

"That's your professional opinion?" I asked, testy.

"I'm not paid to have opinions, man," he said.

"Nor is he a professional," the other opined.

The pair reminded me of Porknuckle and Schticklefish but without the smarts. Part of me wanted to send them out for mead just to see what they'd come back with.

Instead, I took a swing.

I'm not sure why, maybe their willful ignorance just pissed me off. The punch didn't connect with either orderly. The one closest did something with his hands and the air such that my fist thudded into the wall. Like clockwork, his accomplice pulled my coat around my shoulders, locking me into an ersatz straight jacket, then pushed me to my knees with some sort of Vulcan death grip on the back of my neck.

Instead of kicking my ass, which they were entirely entitled to do at this point, the one who offered me Mac's shoes spoke in a soothing voice and said, "Emotions run high at times like this. It's okay, let's just calm down and breathe."

The other inhaled deeply and gestured that I do the same, which I did, seeing as I had caught a break and no longer had dental insurance.

"That's right, just breathe," he continued. "You feeling better?"

I nodded and the death grip eased. I felt like a bad dog. The guy pulled me to my feet, fixed my coat and patted me on the shoulders. They clearly had what Annika called "spiritual centers." I apparently had a spiral.

"You better have that hand looked at," the breathing coach said. I looked down as a trickle of blood ran off my knuckle and onto my boot.

"Thanks," I managed to say as my breathing grew more excited. "And sorry."

They just smiled, zipped up Mac's bag and wheeled him through the door.

I collapsed in Mac's chair, the very spot he breathed his last breath and tried to catch my own. The adrenaline seemed to kick in a bit late. I tried to shake it off but I was anxious, speedy. Clearly, my fight-or-flight principle was out of whack. I felt nauseous. And sore. I scanned Mac's room for something to wrap my hand in but wasn't impressed with the level of hygiene in the place. Instead, I plucked a page from my reporter's notebook and cupped it around the edge of my hand. The slow flow of blood blotted the paper like a Japanese rising sun.

When I was satisfied that the tiny cut above my little finger had begun to scab, I got up to toss the page in the trash, which I figured to be under the sink like in every other place in America.

And it was. So was Mac's collection of precious newspapers. Resting atop the tuna fish cans and empty bottles of Audacious Red was the entire run of President Dewey's first week in office. I pulled the lot from the garbage and bundled them under my arm, including "Dewey Wins." At the very least, I had a reason to remember my eBay password.

More importantly, I had something to hang onto perhaps the way the Mac did. Why would Mac decide to start his Spring cleaning today? Or was it someone else? The caller, the voice. Did I draw her here? I couldn't stand the thought

of being the connective tissue to someone else's death —
again.

"Are you stealing his recycling?" Jude asked as he shook
a handful of Lost Buttons candies into his palm. Framed
in the doorway he looked small and I reminded myself he
was just a kid to whom death was just an abstract notion.
For that matter, to me, life was just an abstract notion, so
we somehow made a complementary team. And we had to
run.

I pressed the sheaf of newspapers against Jude's jacket.

"Put these in your coat."

"We are stealing the recycling," he said.

"No, we're not. We're reporting. You want to be Jimmy
Olsen, right?"

"Sure, but this is more like we're gonna make papier-
mâché," he said.

I pushed another couple of yellowed editions onto Jude
who sequestered them as best he could inside his blazer, as
its straining brass button looked about to join the candy
Jude dropped on the floor.

"I feel like a piñata," Jude said.

"Let's go. We've got to hurry."

I hustled Jude toward the door. The half a bale of
newsprint bloating his uniform caused him to waddle.

"This is how the mafia drowns newspaper people isn't it?"
Jude joked.

"It's the impact of hitting the water that kills you, not
drowning."

Jude stared at me a moment

"Um, what are you talking about?" he finally asked.

I realized that my mind was leaking.

"Nevermind," I said.

* * *

Five years ago, on assignment at the U, a young marine biologist thought it would be helpful for me to know what happens to bodies lost at sea. He knew my legend. He knew 1K was never found. He tried in his miserable academic way to help.

"Usually, they wash up to the surface in a few months," he explained, adjusting his hip glasses. "Internal gasses build up and the body, or what's left of it, will float like an inner tube. Barring that, certain marine life will eat a corpse, though these are usually smaller, scavenger animals, not the larger animals of prey in the Bay. Sharks and orca prefer to catch their own dinners – they prefer fresh meat. Otherwise, natural decomposition occurs with bacteria and other organisms breaking down the tissues over time. Of course, exposure to salt water and sun help."

"Salt water and sun," I repeated. "Sounds like a Beach Boys song."

And with that, I left whistling a tune. At least I could pretend, a mermaid found a swimming lad…

14.

Heave Ho

For a weekday morning, the offices of the Lumaville blog were suspiciously quiet. Albeit the child journalists and other riffraff usually drifted in just in time to check their social media accounts before knocking off for an overpriced lunch at whatever vogue restaurant was gentrifying the strip below that week. Beer bottles lined the large window sills like in a shooting gallery. An antique door that had been artfully retrofitted as a conference table was littered with Chinese takeout boxes with chopsticks poking out like antennae.

A thin cloud of gnats hovered over the remains of vegetarian chow mein and mock Kung Pao chicken. A lanky young man in a sweater vest and freshly pasted hair half-heartedly swept red plastic cups into an industrial trash bag. His forearm was bandaged. Fucking Edwyn.

"You missed the party," Adriane said from her desk.

"I wasn't invited."

"Mystery solved," she said.

She looked pretty haggard and it occurred to me that the only reason she was in the office was because she had slept there. She looked a little drunk still.

"And you're here why?"

"The centenarian story," I said. "It's gotten complicated."

"Go on," Adriane said with a woozy glare.

"He's dead. I suspect foul play."

Adriane stared at me. Then she started to giggle. Her trilling voice gave into great peals of laughter punctuated by hiccups. Then she went straight-faced and put her palms flat on the desk. Her eyes went distant and focused as if she could see through me.

I knew what was going to happen next – the hiccups were the give away. On instinct, I grabbed her wastebasket and spun her around on her chair and put the can to her face as I gathered her hair with my other hand. She was pliant all the way through, even up to the moment it all came spilling out of her bitchy pout in great heaving sloshes.

Chow mein and microbrew. And four years of college too.

That's when I knew she would be a great editor someday.

After a few more spasms she leaned back into her seat but it rolled away and her ass hit the hardwood floor with a bounce. She didn't attempt to recover but rather rolled into a ball beneath her desk.

I marched the garbage to the far end of the spacious office and emptied it out the second story window. I fetched some napkins and a stainless steel water bottle from a random desk.

"Tell me more," Adriane half spat as she coughed into a napkin. I uncapped the water for her and she took a cautious sip.

"There's a stolen phone and a game called 'The Knights of Skeldaria.' And a kid from a parallel universe," I said as I pulled Jude's phone from my pocket and showed her the sticker on the back. I pressed it into her sweaty palm.

"Where's the kid?"

"In my car outside."

"Wowza. You're sure in a heap of shit," she groaned.

"For the sake of the story," I said and I actually meant it. Adriane nodded then closed her eyes as she folded up like a duckling.

"You're past deadline."

"Just need a few more days."

She started giggling again but stabilised herself for fear of another deluge. "Did you sexually harass Edwyn? He said..."

"He's flattering himself."

"He does that," Adriane said, then smiled, "Back off, he's mine."

I looked up and across the floor spied eavesdropping Edwyn. He shrugged, somehow satisfied with this latest development. I considered us even.

Adriane slid the phone back to me.

"Easter egg," she said.

I looked at her, confused. She rolled her eyes and passed out.

I pulled the orange sweater off the back of her chair and draped it over her shoulders. I didn't hover for a thank you, which I think she would've appreciated.

* * *

Edwyn stopped me at the door.

"There's Easter eggs in the 'Knights of Skeldaria,'" he said. "That's what she meant. Little hidden portals the programmers put in that allow you to level up and shit. All the FMRL brand games have them."

"How do you know?"

"It's my beat – I write the game blog," he said. He looked hurt that I didn't know his curriculum vitae.

"I thought you were launching a startup?"

He turned red.

"I won't talk. We're square," I said. "So, these portals are in the game?"

"In every game, programmers put portals in so you can jump around the universe. For testing purposes. In one scenario, you kill the Willogen and get to meet the Wizard," Edwyn explained. "Or, you can just cheat using the Easter eggs and meet him anyway."

"Meet the Wizard?"

"The founder of FMRL," he said. "Cameron Block."

My turn to go red. I wanted to believe that I felt guilty for leaving Jude in the Mini longer than I'd promised but it was really because I hated Cameron Block.

* * *

This much I knew: Cam had downshifted into games after his first start-up failed and lost him and his Russian mobster investors a shitload of money. He was back in school, not studying, but doing research and spinning popular apps out of what was once the Pataphysics Department (when active, his business had purchased the "naming rights" to the field of study as a PR stunt, which also netted an honorary degree for Cam and an open door with the beneficiaries in the department. I think they were just glad to remove the name "Slutnik" from the corridors).

In the past decade, Cam had made a name for himself as a tech bad boy who curried respect in academic circles by innovating patentable technologies, which he gifted to the university.

Magazine features followed. I wrote one. My last one, in fact. It featured cleft-chinned Cam mugging for the camera with a little girl riding his shoulders clutching a tattered teddy bear. "How this man's Killer App saved this Lost Little Girl's Life," read the headline. The events connecting the playboy technologist and the Goldilocks lookalike was tenuous, but a savvy publicist connected the dots and I went merrily down the trail like like a greedy bird eating bread crumbs.

There was once a movie in the works. But now, apparently, there were mobile games. He was, as they say, "Just one of those guys." Why I was not "one of those guys" haunted me. It was like we were all playing musical chairs and, while he was making a play for the throne, I was bitching about the music. The modernist hangover we inherited made me believe this was somehow important. It's been a costly pose.

15.
Big Box

Back in the parking lot, I was vaguely relieved that the car and Jude were still there as I'd left them. I opened the car door, slid into the the driver's seat and drew Jude's phone out of my pocket again.

"You're not going to try the app again, are you?" he said, finishing the fast food fries I plied him with to stay in the car and ward away meter maids.

"No, I'm looking at the contacts. Sometimes people put themselves in their own phone. If they lose it, someone can find them that way," I lied. I had a hunch.

I thumbed through the index of names. There were only a few and most ended in a vowel or a Y (whatever that meant) or were preceded with honorifics like "Doctor" and "Professor" or followed by "esquire." Whoever's phone this was, they were thorough. Anal, really.

Bingo. "Cameron Block," tech star burnout, faux academician and gaming mogul. What was he doing in this kid's hot phone? I thought about calling him but realized I'd have the drop if I just showed up. And I knew where to go – where I last saw him at Lumaville U. Pataphysics Department. I beelined for the campus.

"You know a guy named Cameron Block?" I asked Jude.

He shook his head, which made me like him all the more. I did a U-turn.

"Where are we going? I thought we were on assignment."

"We are, it's just that I have another lead I want to check on real quick."

Then, I realized that I needed a sitter – not the first time in my life, but the first time I needed one for someone who wasn't me cruising for company on the eve of a bender.

I figured I had two cards to play, both wild: I could hit up Crysta the Barista or Detective Shane. The former would cost me about thirty bucks and some self-respect. The latter could lose me my star pupil if I wasn't clever about it.

I chose card three: a less complicated route.

"You wanna go to the movies?" I asked Jude.

"Hell yeah."

"Excellent. But first we have to run an errand."

* * *

A husky rent-a-cop stood outside the big box store, still, like a cigar store Indian. When he did move, it was to acknowledge everyone who entered with a slight nod of his head, which was a minor triumph since he didn't have much of a neck. Inside, was an air hangar-sized IOU to the power company. The amount of electricity wasted on illuminating screens and things that go thump, thump, thump in the night was staggering. And noisy. And air-conditioned within a few degrees of freezing. I imagined working there was like living in a pinball machine that doubled as a meat locker.

Jude seemed to know his way around and alighted at a game console like a lunamoth. Kids navigate these kinds of places by instinct while their guardians make a slow wade in search of anyone in a blue polo shirt and a name tag.

The mobile phones had their own kiosk near the center of the store. Jude seemed content destroying robots in the futurescape of some video game so I let him continue his target practice for the eventual uprising.

I placed Jude's phone atop the glass counter in front of a young, dark guy with thick black eyebrows that creased his forehead like an old fashioned banker's visor. He looked down at the phone with clinical detachment.

"Broken?"

"Not sure. It's my kid's," I lied. "I'm curious where he got it – I've never seen this model before."

The clerk picked it up and turned it in his long, bony hands. He tapped the sticker and said, "The Willogen from the Knight of Skeldaria. I can never beat that thing." Then he did some kind of tech geek sleight of hand and a panel effortlessly popped off the back. He pinched it between his thumb and forefinger and squinted at some kind of hieroglyphics on its inside.

"Hmm," he observed.

"Is that a good 'hmm' or a bad 'hmm,'" I asked.

"It's just a 'hmm-hmm,'" he said without looking up. "It's definitely jailbroken. Looks like an aftermarket hack job on a..."

He stood up straight and did 180 degree scan of the room, like a lighthouse beam scanning a bay. As his eyes passed by mine, it was if he looked right through me.

"Or it's a prototype," he said. "Which means its hot."

"It does get warm after a bit," I agreed.

"No, man. It's stolen."

"Well, I know that much. That tweener over there came home with it," I said. "I'm trying to make it right with whomever..."

"I mean stolen from the lab," he said. "You could sell this

to a tech blog for a few grand."

I too stood up straight and scanned the room.

"No shit." My blood was beginning to flow again. "Which one?"

He put the phone back on the counter but kept his hand on top of it.

"I could help you," he offered with a knowing frown, then his eyes darted over my shoulder. "That your kid?"

I whipped my head around.

Jude had made his way to the video camera displays and was busy pointing a camera on himself as dozens of Judes peered back from the flat screens surrounding us like a mosaic. Each image of his face was a different size and in a slightly different hue. It was like looking at the world through the eyes of a fly.

"Hey, little man, you're not ready for primetime yet," the clerk called to him.

A couple of customer service reps ran over to the camera and reset the signal so that all the TVs played a football game as Jude slipped down the aisle.

"Sorry about that," I said. The clerk nodded. He then raised an eyebrow. He returned the phone to me after a few more expert swipes.

"You better ask this chick if she's offering a reward," he said. "But I bet it won't be half as much as a blog bounty." On the screen was contact information for someone named "Prof. Alexandria Ashe."

"Who's that?" I asked.

"That's the registered owner," he said. "I unlocked some securities permissions. I hope you don't mind. And you're right. The thing does get hot."

"Why is that?"

"It's radiation. And bad for you, so don't hold it up to your head too much. Or your brains will liquify," he said.

"So, what are you going to do?"

"Give it back to the rightful owner."

"Fair enough," he shrugged. "Mind if I take a picture of it?"

I nodded and he snapped two quick shots, front and back of the phone, on his own device. He slid it back to me across the glass counter.

"You're probably making the right choice," he said. "Corporate espionage is a federal offense. Besides, you look like you could use the karma."

I put the phone back in my pocket and nodded adieu.

I found Jude in the car stereo section where dozens of systems were mounted on the wall like hunting trophies.

"Let's split, I have a lead."

He hopped to it, eager to leave. However, every five feet some techno whizbang would catch his eye and he'd have to investigate, like dogs sniffing fire hydrants. "Checking their pee-mail," Annika once joked.

I beat Jude outside. When he crossed the threshold a horrible store alarm went off. I looked back and in a flash the no-neck security guard had dropped his baseball glove hands on Jude's shoulders.

"Hand it over," he grunted.

A small semi-circle of onlookers had instantly developed. They shook their heads and muttered between themselves like a Greek chorus on a smoke break. Jude avoided eye contact with me, so to prove a point – what, I'm not sure – I let him dangle while the guard did his business.

"Give me what you got," the guard insisted.

"Did you take something?" I asked.

"No!" Jude spat.

The alarm grated our ears with the same sad song as European cop cars. It sounded like someone whining "Nina, Nina!" into an electrolarynx.

118

"Are you sure you didn't take anything?" I pressed.

"Yes."

He looked up at me and shrugged. He was cute but he wasn't cute enough to make this scene go away, not least of which because the store's "loss prevention officer," a slight woman who looked like she sprayed her perfect ringlets with "can-do spirit," sprinted through the door with a portable phone in her hand.

"This your kid?" she asked crisply. I looked at Jude who looked away. "Little shits like these cost this store tens of thousands of dollars a year in loss," she said. I knew she had an arsenal of facts and figures she was dying to let spill but I didn't want to give her the chance.

"He didn't take anything," I said. I looked to Jude again to make sure he wasn't lying. I couldn't tell.

"Well, someone took something. You hear the alarm? Did you take something?" she pointed her phone at me. "One of you set off our alarm. And I've got the police on speed dial! You're one finger away from a free ride downtown."

Sounded like a bad pick up line but I didn't mention it. Jude and I didn't need the heat. He'd end up in the maze of social services and I'd be busted for everything from harboring a runaway to obstruction of justice, to who knows what back-asswards law Detective Shane could dredge up. I played my hand.

"Pat us down," I challenged her as I brought my elbows to my ears. "Check our pockets. We didn't take anything, right, Jude?"

Jude squirmed in the security guard's clutch.

"Right, Jude?" I pressed. Jude kept his eyes on his shoes.

The door flung open and the heavy-browed clerk from the mobile department hung halfway out its frame.

"Hey, turn off that phone!" he called to me as he patted his pocket, then twirled his finger in the air. Nina, Nina! I got what he meant. I turned off Jude's phone and the alarm quit the moment the screen went dead.

The security guard looked to the loss prevention officer who tossed her curls off her forehead and quietly said "Sorry for the confusion." She snapped her portable phone into a holster on her belt and sashayed past the eyebrows.

Jude brushed the guard's ham hocks off his shoulders and moved to my side.

"Told you," he said, exasperated.

"Hey, I believed you, didn't I?" I said, though I think he could I tell I had merely made a calculated guess.

I looked up and caught a quick head nod from the clerk as he ducked back through the door.

Karma.

16.
FMRL

My world view isn't jaundiced, it's just yellow from age. Like the pages of a cheap paperback or nicotine-stained fingers, or a Simpson. This is how I know too much about the dark side of Swedish genre flicks and that the campus cinema was showing a matinee of some bullshit I forced myself to love before it was cool. Buntel Eriksson's *Den Plastspion – The Plastic Spy*.

We were parked outside the cinemas.

"Ah, 'Den Plastspion' is playing, ok?" I announced with all the enthusiasm I could muster.

"Ok," Jude responded. Then he had second thoughts. "What's it about?"

"You'll like it," I said. "It's got boobs."

"How many?"

"Two. That's the usual," I said. "It's an art film, which is about as close as a kid your age should get to porn."

"It's in Swedish? I don't speak Swedish."

"Hmm, so I've overestimated you again," I said. "Don't worry, there are subtitles. You can read can't you?"

"Not Swedish."

"If you get bored you can harass the student ushers – make them earn those three units for standing around in the dark."

I parked in the back lot of the U and decided to risk not paying the ten dollar parking fee. I hastened Jude out of the car. We cut across the campus, dodging the sinewy joggers and pear-shaped girls with dyed hair and clothes two sizes too tight, which somehow worked on them. I couldn't see it but somewhere a drum circle was thumping away. Bongos always sounded to me like the soundtrack that accompanies human sacrifice. In this case, it would be Jude, or at least his cinematic innocence. It was a calculated forfeit that I, as an accredited member of the media, was obliged to make.

It must have been "club day." Throughout the campus, various student-manned booths promised everything from business networking to the secrets of meditation and ashtanga yoga. Religious groups proliferated around the edges – post-Protestant proselytizers in short sleeve button-up shirts and skinny black ties. They were either working for Jesus or between sets for their ska band.

Parked at a table in front of the film studies department was a lonely-looking guy with a scraggly beard, wild eyes and a hand-lettered sign that read, "Hey, Ladies, join my cult!" While I was studying him, two women actually approached and he went to work on them with a broad smile and a couple of brochures.

"See, that's how you do it," I said to Jude. "You need a brochure."

"I need money."

"That too."

"No. To get into the movies."

I gave Jude a ten dollar bill. The last of my available cash.

"Can I get popcorn?"

"I don't think it's that kind of place. You can get coffee. Bad coffee."

"I don't drink coffee. I'm a kid."

"Kids drink coffee in Europe. Besides, you're not a kid, you're a grown up with a glandular disorder. You might have to fake your age to get in. 'Adult themes' and all."

Jude squinted his doe-brown eyes.

"I thought you said this was an art film."

"If anyone asks, say you're 18. A short 18. But don't say you're a midget. It's offensive. The term is 'little person.' Use it only as a last resort.'"

"That sounds even more offensive," he said, palming the tenner.

"Tell it to the A.P. Style manual," I said. I took out Jude's phone and thumbed through the contacts. "Also, I'm keeping this. I like the sticker."

"I figured."

"While you're in there, I have to find someone."

Jude looked at me.

"Who's that?" he asked.

"The bad guy. I think."

Jude nodded, looked at his shoes.

"I need to tell you something. About the bad guy."

"For crying out loud, kid, why didn't you tell me before?"

He gave me a hard looking over. A stone sank in my gut.

"It's not me, is it?"

"If it was, I wouldn't be worried," Jude said.

"It worries you more that I might be the good guy, doesn't it?"

"Kind of. Yes," said Jude. He had an idea and tried it on me with a cocked eyebrow. "Okay. You know how Kal-El was sent to Earth before Krypton blew up?"

"You mean Superman?" I said. The Christopher Reeve clip reel unspooled in my mind. "Got it, right, baby Superman, sent here by his parents."

"Yeah, his parents," Jude echoed. "Because it was safer for

him to be here. Rather than home."

"You're saying you're Superman?"

"What? No."

"You're Superbaby?"

"Ugh!" he spat, frustrated. "She said you'd be like this!"

"Who?" I said. "And like what?"

"Nevermind."

He huffed and turned to leave. Despite myself, I knew I had to say something, anything reassuring.

"Come here, Jude – if that is indeed your real name. I know you're more scared than you're letting on. And despite being a natty dresser and whip smart, you're just a kid and you need help. It's hard to ask for help at your age. That was brave of you. You keep that up and got this thing half beat."

Jude bit his lip and nodded.

"You think I'm brave?"

"Of course I do…"

I mussed his hair until I could think of something else to say.

"…The Force is strong around you."

"That's not how it goes," he said as he shook his head and walked, stooped-shouldered, into the box office. He looked back and I gave him a thumbs up. He did the same and stepped inside.

If memory served, I had precisely ninety-eight minutes of total-running-time to figure out how Cameron Block, the caller on the phone, old dead Mac and this strange child had become the shapers of my professional future.

* * *

The Pataphysics Department was in a handsome building, modern in a manner that recalled the evil lairs of James

Bond villains or 70s sci-fi – all angles and cool concrete offset by terrible outdoor sculpture. In this case, it was a bulbous, twenty-foot obelisk that snickering faculty called the "corndog" but students simply called "The Dick."

Inside, it was all air-conditioned bustle. In the center of the foyer was a bronze bust of Alfred Jarry, the imperial-mustached French charlatan and artist, who invented the discipline of Pataphysics, a term few knew beyond a passing reference in "Maxwell's Silver Hammer" by The Beatles. "Joan was quizzical..." etc. It was the science of the "imaginary solutions and the laws governing exceptions" and it was a crock of shit. Consequently, it was quite popular with students, who emptied their classrooms, their brains sizzling like Pop Rocks with notions that were beautiful, abstract and utterly useless 50 feet outside of campus.

I found a stairwell and began my climb to Cam's ivory tower. On the second floor I found a directional sign that read "Future Media Research Lab" and followed the arrows to a lab a couple of turns away. The door was made of thick steel for no reason other than to appease the architect's muse. On it were the initials FMRL, which I read aloud. That's when I realized it was a pun. Clever, Mr. Block, I thought to myself.

I decided I should knock on the door before I figured out a reason to join Jude at the matinee. Or the campus pub.

No one answered. Damn shame, I thought. I'd have to get a beer and try again tomorrow. As I was turning away the door flung wide.

"Daedalus Howell!" said a well-coiffed man who looked about five years younger, thinner and richer than me. "It's still 'Daedalus Howell,' right? Or back to Kit?"

Big laughter. My gut turned in on itself like a Klein bottle.

Cameron pulled me into a great heap of a hug, probably

so I could feel how taut he was under his fitted shirt. He invited me into the lab, which looked like a cross between Dr. Frankenstein's workspace and a trendy eatery. The furniture was all low and swank and the room's perimeter was lined with lockers that looked salvaged from an army barracks before being "aesthetically recontextualized." So-called "Edison bulbs" with naked filaments glowing orange hung from stainless steel fixtures, pinned high up on the ceiling.

"This is it, man — it's not much but it's work," Cam beamed.

"What work exactly do you do?" I asked, only half-kidding. He laughed again and pulled me by the arm to a sitting area with shag carpet and cube-shaped ottomans strewn with lime-colored cushions.

"Have a seat," he said. "Espresso?"

"Yes, please," I said.

He looked over his shoulder and snapped. Holy shit, he has servants? I thought, until a small vacuum cleaner-sized robot rolled over. It stopped in front of us and started to emit steam. It was either going to explode or eventually put baristas out of business. For the moment, either outcome was fine with me. A hatch opened and a tray emerged from the bot with two perfectly deployed espressos on it. Cam's smile was genuine, childlike. Nothing like the churlish grimace I'd come to loathe in school.

"Starbucks is going to hate you," I said.

"Wrong. Starbucks is going to love me. No labor issues, no health benefits, no attitude."

"The attitude is what we're paying for," I countered. I was losing so I pivoted. "So, is this what you do now? Coffee?"

Cam smirked, then squared his big dreamy eyes on me. He tented his fingers and said: "Disruption. That's what I do now."

Disruption. That was one of our keywords at the blog a few weeks ago. Cam searched for purpose and found it in Google Trends. Asshole.

"So, you're still –" Cam flitted his fingers in the air as if he were imitating a spider. He was actually imitating me typing.

"Yeah, man. That's why I'm here. I'm on a story," I said.

Cam cooled a little. Then I remembered why.

"Not about me, I hope," he said, peering through his well shaped eyebrow.

"No, not at all, nothing like that."

"Because last time wasn't so pleasant for either of us," he reminded.

Long before 1K leapt off the bridge and eons before Annika split, Cam was launching his first start-up and I did a profile on him for a slick business rag. Instead of the cheerleading he and his investor pals expected, and frankly my editor expected as well, I did a sort of Gonzo piece on what it's like to run up bar tabs, play Fusbol and bed publicists, all on the venture capitalist's dime. It wasn't inaccurate but it wasn't pretty. Cam's firm threatened a libel suit until he talked them down. I had forgotten the whole affair. It was under a different byline after all.

"So, who is this for anyway?"

"The piece?" I asked then took a sip of espresso to buy myself time to think of an answer. Wasn't enough. "No one. I mean me – it's for a book." I didn't want to explain that I was one missed deadline from being replaced by a few lines of code – code he'd probably write.

"A book?" appraised Cam. "Ambitious. A book on what?"

I punted.

"Easter eggs," I said.

Cameron Block smiled his wolfish smile, the one he practiced in mirrors, honed on coeds and levitated over single malt scotches with investors. All the better to chew up the media, I thought.

I put Jude's phone on the glass coffee table. Cam regarded it a moment, expressionless.

"You know what this is?"

"It's a phone," he said. "So, are you writing a user's manual?"

He sounded like he might be serious. I might be better off if he was right. Technical writers are the cockroaches of the writing racket. Survivors. And I mean that in the best sense of the word 'racket.'

"It's not the phone that's interesting so much as its provenance, I suspect."

"Go on," he said.

"It's got your game on it. 'The Knights of Skeldaria.'"

Cam leaned back in his chair. He ran his fingers through his two-hundred dollar haircut and smirked.

"You know how many phones have 'The Knights of Skeldaria' on them? They can't make zeroes fast enough to keep up," Cam said. He looked at me and counted to three slowly. "There we go, ten thousand more."

He picked up the phone.

"Don't play it."

"Why not?"

"I'm not sure what it does but the kid I took it from is scared shitless."

"What, the Willogen?" Cam laughed.

"Professor Ashe."

Cam stopped laughing.

"What does this have to do with Professor Ashe?" he asked.

"It's her phone," I said.

"Are you returning it?"

"No, I want to know what it does and what it's really

all about. And what the hell does infinity-dash-one mean, anyway?" I said. The espresso was beginning to work on me.

Cam put the phone down and considered it a moment while rubbing the back of his neck.

"Professor Ashe was a part of a league of acid-dropping kooks who were trying to link quantum mechanics to paranormal activity, ESP, ghosts and the multiverse. Only the last had any merit," Cam explained. He waited for me to raise an eyebrow. Finally, I bit.

"Multiverse?"

"Parallel universes, man." He snapped his fingers and the barista-bot began steaming again. "I'm addicted to this shit. You want another?"

I hesitated, which, to a man like Cam, was an invitation for swift, definitive action. "Have another," he advised. "You look like you need it."

"What I need is this story."

"Yeah, so, how do I know you're not plotting some hit piece on the Pataphysics department. We get enough guff for being pseudoscience. The last thing we need is someone proving it," Cam said. "It messes with our funding. Not that we're hurting, obviously. FMRL is doing quite well."

Obviously. The robot served me more coffee. It lingered after I took my cup. I looked up at Cam for the next move.

"Tip it. It wants a tip."

I gave it a little shove, enough to get one of its three wheels off the ground.

"I can see that you're popular at cafes."

I sighed and put my last crumpled dollar onto the robot's tray. It finally left.

"Okay. You wanna know about the multiverse?"

I nodded and pulled out my own phone to record Cam quotes. He shook his head.

"This is on background," he said. "I'll tell you when it gets juicy enough to quote. Fair enough?"

"Fair enough." I put the phone back in my pocket. It was still recording.

"Okay, the multiverse," he said before thumbing the screen of his phone. "The multiverse is the set of infinite or finite possible universes, including the historical universe we consistently experience, that together comprise everything that exists."

"Did you just look that up on Wikipedia?"

"Yes, I did. And?"

"Dude, I could have done that."

"You could've but you didn't and that makes all the difference doesn't it?" he fanned his hands out like a showroom model to remind me just how different our lives had become. "Of course, that's in this universe. In another, who knows what kind of asshole I am."

"So, this isn't the asshole universe?" I said. "You had me."

Cam's tongue prodded one of his unusually sharp canines as his lips curled into a shit-eating grin. "You know who you oughta talk to..."

He sprung to his designer tennies and beckoned me to follow him.

We went through a pair of double doors at the end of the lab and started down a long hall. Throughout, various machines and their makers wandered along.

A tall student passed us in the hall as he inched along what looked like a heavy stack of traffic lights with camera lenses where the lights should be. "She in there?" Cam asked him.

"Where else?" he said with a shrug. Just over his shoulder was a red door with a small window in it. Cam didn't knock. He leaned into the knob and rolled into the room, holding the door wide for me...

Sonofabitch.

* * *

Annika Strang was the definition of grace under pressure. Or any other cliche used to sell underarm deodorant or a waterproof watch. It wasn't that she looked great (the way that exes always do) or that she clearly had her lab coat tailored so that it tapered at the waist – it was the plain prettiness of a catalog model she affected when still. For some reason, this looked like grace to me, if a bit mannequin-like, especially since she didn't even blink when the muzzle of the Webley-Fosbery revolver tapped the lens of her glasses.

On the other side of it was a crude bric-a-brac of hydraulic limbs, cables and gears connected to an artificial intelligence unit apparently gone rogue.

It was a robot stick-up. Albeit one with what appeared to be a World War One-era antique pistol. Cam ripped the fire extinguisher from the wall and walloped the robot's arm, snapping it in two and buying Annika enough time to pull its electrical cord from a nearby socket. The robot shuddered and folded into a heap upon the floor.

Annika knelt down and picked up the gun.

"He buys them off the Internet," she said matter-of-factly as she crossed the lab, pivoting past androids in various states of completion. She unloaded the gun and tossed it in a drawer with the others. The bullets rolled off her palm like marbles into her lab coat pocket.

Cam turned to me. "That was JCN. Pronounced 'Jason.'"

"What is he supposed to be, a security robot or something?" I asked lamely.

"Nanny, actually. We've had some bugs."

Annika sighed. "For crissakes, he's a robot. Doesn't anybody do background checks when selling guns?" She knelt to collect

JCN's fingers, which were on the floor, splayed like a bouquet of corkscrews.

"The real question is whose credit card is he using?" Cam said.

"No, the real question, Cam, is what the fuck is he doing here?" Annika said as she dipped her rectangular glasses at me. I was waiting for her to acknowledge me. It was almost worth the wait.

"Uh, hello, Annie," I said. "How are things?"

The words made her wince.

"I almost got murdered by an erector set. That's how 'things' are."

"You're welcome, by the way," Cam said to her coyly. Annika smiled at him.

The adrenaline of the moment waned enough for me to feel my bruised ego again. What was my ex doing working at FMRL with Cameron Block? And more importantly... Was she fucking him?

17.
The Penultimate Integer

Outside, the horde of students had thinned and a crisp wind blew through the campus. With it came a whirlwind of leaves, a missing persons flyer (Professor Ashe) and a foreboding sense that I should've left well enough alone.

Cam led Annika and me heedlessly through the intra-campus traffic, which he instinctively knew would stop for him. I wasn't so sure about myself — I managed to get hit by my own parked car once. Annika, however, also had traffic stopping powers and could still inspire rubbernecking. This was not in spite of so much because of the fact that she too had crested her 40s. She had good looks the way critics refer to certain films as "sleepers;" she warmed up on the eyes like glow plugs. And then like a diesel, it was hard to stop. I knew what Cam saw in her (world weary wit, Scandinavian reserve, the ability to drink) but I had no idea what she saw in him, besides, you know, the wealth, power and good looks. Apparently, everything depicted in 80s rom-coms was a lie.

Near the base of The Dick was a squat brick building, obscured by verdant ivy except for a well-worn wooden door in the middle. Cam swung it wide and we entered the

Faculty Club.

A young man who had the schnozz of a woodpecker and styled his hair to complete the profile, looked up from a ledger at the podium and needled me with his eyes.

Cam, always good at social cues, said, "He's our guest." This did little to get the kid to forgive the fact that an interloper had made it into the University's inner sanctum. Clubby. I didn't think that in Lumaville this sort of joint existed, with its Old World class distinctions burnished into the dark hardwood paneling, overstuffed chairs and all. If smoking hadn't fallen out of fashion, they would've issued velvet jackets and meerschaum pipes at the door.

The woodpecker sat us in a booth and three pints materialized atop our table within seconds. Cam waved at a plump fellow a few tables away, then flicked his thumb at his quarry. "He owed me. Lost a bet on string theory." Cam raised his glass: "Cheers! First time – breakthrough. Second time – serious lapse in security."

We connected glasses.

"Are you referring to our guest or our former robot?" Annika deadpanned.

"Haven't decided yet," he said, then took a sip.

I also had a slug but when we all put our pints down, somehow mine was already half–empty, or half–full, depending.

"Tell me you're not going to write about this," she said. "The robot, et cetera."

"Not my beat," I said.

"He's doing a book about mobile phones," Cam said "And the multiverse."

"There's an app for that. I hear." I said. It was lame joke but it did the job. Annika looked briefly at Cam, who kept his eyes on me. Classic.

"A book? Well," Annika nodded. "I flattered myself and

thought you were here to see me. About the couch. Or the money you owe me."

"We better come clean and tell him everything," Cam said with a feigned sigh.

Annika nodded.

"We're dating," Cam blurted.

The words landed hard and heavy on my stomach and I was instantly hot and clammy, as if in a sweat lodge. Annika shook her head, disapproving.

"We're not," she said. And into the ice pool. My psyche didn't have enough tensile strength to do this yin and yang shit and I let myself be annoyed.

"Fucking A, you guys, I just need some background, not your tawdry horseshit." Twenty years I know these people and we're all still a bunch of assholes.

"There's nothing tawdry about it," said Annika. She realized she sounded defensive and pushed her thumb against her brow as if to steady herself lest she fall down Cam's semantic claptrap. "What do you want to know about the multiverse?"

"Was that what Professor Ashe was working on?"

"You mean before she disappeared?" asked Annika. "In a word, yes. But indirectly."

Cam cleared his throat.

"What she means is that Ashe was part of a team, a holdover from the sixties that worked on wormholes, time travel…"

"Your basic hippie shit," I said, just as old Mac had described it.

"Sure, that," Cam said. He hated his flow being hijacked. "They practiced what they called Fungible Fysiks, with two Fs."

"And it worked?"

"No, it didn't. Like most Baby Boomer mindfucks, it

ended badly. Not Manson-bad but bad enough. However, it did lead to a field of study that did work. You see, Ashe isn't missing. Not as I see it. I mean, she's not here but that doesn't mean she's not there."

"You're beginning to lose me," I said. But I was lying.

Annika leaned in.

"What if she was able to open a portal and enter a parallel universe?"

"What if?"

Annika scrunched up her face and shook her head at my apparent failure to appreciate the awesomeness of it all. She was like this whenever she returned from Burning Man, caked in playa dust and ranting like a mad woman about the free pottery workshops for rural teens she wanted to launch just as soon as she learned how to make pottery, bought a kiln, took a shower and the Ecstasy wore off.

"If Ashe made it over can't you see how it would fundamentally change our understanding of reality?"

Yep. She drank the Kool-Aid. She needed to believe, to have faith in the premise, whereas I had already met a couple of parallel people and it seemed to bring nothing but heartache.

"So, how is the multiverse real and time travel isn't?"

"The grandfather paradox," Annika said. "You go back in time and kill your grandfather before he meets your grandmother, hence your parent isn't born, hence you're not born. How is it then that you were able to go back in time at all to kill the man, if, in the timeline of events that led to your birth, you were eradicated by your act?"

"I couldn't."

"Certainly. It violates causality," she said. "But that's only if you're on a linear timeline."

"And we're not?" I asked. Annika shook her head. If only someone could explain this to the Editrix I'd no longer have deadline issues, I thought.

"Instead of a movie that plays in one direction, imagine a movie that plays in all directions."

"Got it. You invented Netflix two-point-O," I joked but they were too enamored with their explication on life, the multiverse and everything to laugh. Instead, Cam got tagged into the ring.

"Okay, remember those Choose Your Own Adventure books? You'd read through, making several decisions along the way – do you slay the dragon, yes or no? If no, go to X, if yes, go to Y. You'd race through about thirty, forty pages and exhaust that plot line. But you know there's a helluva lot of book left. Hundreds of pages, in fact. You start over. What's germane is that the Many-worlds theory acknowledges all those other pages, all those decisions unmade as existing parallel plots."

"As parallel universes, you mean," I said.

"Exactly," Annika said with a nod. She was back in. "Every quantum outcome is realized. And it's infinite. Everything that could have happened but didn't, does in another universe."

"Now, I don't feel so bad about missing the network broadcast of 'The Day After' as a kid," I said. "Because some other version of me, in some other Lumaville did see it."

"Yes."

"No, you should still feel bad. That was the touchstone for a generation," Cam added. "But, yes, somewhere, somehow, you saw 'The Day After,' though it might not have been 'The Day After' we saw. With infinite worlds, infinite variations. You could wake up in a world where Royal Crown won the Cola wars, the Padres never won the series and the Walrus was Paul."

"The Walrus was Paul," I corrected.

Cam waved his palms in the air, mockingly: "Oooh, see,

you've crossed over."

"If there's infinite universes, how do you get back to the one you came from?" I asked. "How do you know the 'one' is your 'one?'"

"Because it's the one you came from," Annika said.

Her Zen-like answer reminded me of Mac.

"What if you end up in the wrong universe? Is it real or is it Memorex?"

"It's real. It's just not here."

"But you can travel between the two?"

"Between all of them."

"But how?"

"I think you know how," Cam said. "Show her what you've got there, Dade."

I put the phone on the table and our hands hovered above it like it was the planchette atop a Ouija board.

"It's an iPhone," said Annika.

"Look at the apps," he said. "'Knights of Skeldaria.' And someone unlocked a very particular Easter Egg."

Annika's pianist fingers danced over the face of the phone, pulling up the *Knights of Skeldaria* and just as quickly a prompt that looked to me like a numeral eight and a couple of lines.

"What is that?"

"It's one of the game's many Easter Eggs. This one, however, is special. It was Professor Ashe's very own little digital cubby hole," said Annika. "It's a very large number."

"Eight?"

She turned the phone ninety degrees.

"That's a lemniscate."

I blinked.

"An infinity symbol. It reads 'Infinity minus one.' Or as we like to say, 'the Penultimate Integer.'"

I blinked again. Annika sighed. "The number right

before infinity."

As far as spit takes go, mine was minor. I got most of it with a napkin. The rest was on my blazer.

"Are you fucking kidding me?" I said. "The number before infinity? What kind of scam are you guys running here?"

"It's not a scam, it's an equation. Infinity minus one. Professor Ashe was the first to describe it."

"It sounds like grant bait to me," I said.

"More like camouflage. Wait a minute. This is her phone. Where did you get this?"

Cam smiled.

"A kid turned up with it. Found it on the SMART train," I explained.

"When?" Annika asked.

"This week."

Cam crossed his arms and cocked his head.

"You didn't mention a kid. Who is he?"

"His name is Jude," I said.

"You turned him in to the cops I hope. For stealing the phone."

"He got himself pinched but he got away. The thing was the cops couldn't turn up any records on him. It's like he never existed."

"Like he never existed *here*," Cam said.

"Exactly, he's not a missing person. He came out of nowhere."

"No, he came from somewhere but that somewhere was a parallel universe."

"Then why doesn't he have a double here?"

"Parallel only means side by side, not mirror image."

"But parallel lines never meet," I said, the one thing I remembered from geometry.

Cam sighed.

"It's like an 'H,' like your initial. A couple of parallel lines linked by a bridge," he said. "The lines don't touch but the bridge touches both." He tapped on the phone. "That's what this is. The bridge."

"The phone is a bridge?"

"The app, an Easter Egg in the Knights of Skeldaria is the bridge," he said. "And somehow that kid hacked it and got himself from there to here on that bridge. So, that's what you got here, Dade, a kid on a bridge. But you know how to handle that."

Annika's eyes dropped to her pint, embarrassed. I kept mine on Cam's, even as I slugged the last of the ale. I framed him in the blurry lens of the glass bottom. He looked less detestable that way.

"Another round?" Cam said as he rose for the bar.

"Don't you have a robot for that?" I asked.

"We did until Cam smashed it with the fire extinguisher," said Annika.

Annika waited until he was a few paces away. "Sorry. He can be a royal ass."

"Are you fucking him?"

"No and not your business."

"Which means 'yes.'"

"Which means it's not your business."

"You're working for him."

"With him," she corrected. "Are you that jealous that you haven't noticed what an extraordinary situation you're in?"

"That my ex is with my lifelong rival?"

"That's a first — you never spoke of Cam like that when we were together."

"Because I was winning then."

"Anyway," she said, catching herself at the event horizon of the conversational black hole I was already down. "This kid, this boy is part of something amazing and you're witness to it.

"I'm not just witness to it. He knew my name was Kit Fergus."

"What?" She put her beer down. "He knows you?"

"He seems to know someone like me."

"Holy shit," she said. "Where is he now?"

"He's at the campus movie theater watching a Buntel Eriksson flick."

"And the cycle of abuse continues," Annika rued. "Swedish art cinema is bad for kids, you know that, right?"

"That's the least of his troubles. I think your boyfriend already knew about him."

"Why do you say that?"

"Because he used the male pronoun, but I never said Jude was a boy."

"That's a fifty-fifty shot, dear. You're being absurd."

"No more absurd than your robot ordering guns off the Internet. Twice."

Annika fixed her eyes on me as the notion sank in.

* * *

Cam returned with a tray of pints. He almost forgot to turn his thousand-watt smile back on. We each grabbed a glass and, following Cam's lead, raised them. As mine connected with Cam's, he seized the moment and grabbed the phone.

"Professor Ashe is a missing person, Dade. And you have her phone. See how this looks?" he said thumbing the screen before he nonchalantly slipped the phone into his top coat pocket. If the coat had a coat of arms badge on its pocket, the image of a prep school bully would be complete.

"What the fuck, Cam?"

"I'm taking it to the cops," Cam said.

"Cam," I tried to stymie the quaver in my voice. "I really want you to give the phone back to me so I can continue with my business."

Cam leaned back in his chair. If Annika was the least bit annoyed with us, she didn't show it. Instead, she dipped her nose in her pint glass and tried to disappear.

"There is no business, Dade," said Cam. "You're not writing a book — least of all one about mobile phones and the multiverse. I assume you've been recording our conversation on your own phone so you can relive the moment later. Am I right?"

"You're recording us?" Annika asked, her expression one of disgust and disappointment.

I grit my teeth as the adrenaline from anger and shame welled up in my gut.

"Just give the phone back, Cam," Annika said. "People are looking."

She was right, we began to turn heads, including the woodpecker's whose head bobbed to and fro like a ping pong commentator's.

Cam didn't break his icy gaze on me. I did my best to reciprocate. Ever the diplomat, Annika said, "I suggest a new strategy. Let the Wookiee win."

"Wait, which one of us is the Wookiee?" Cam turned to Annika. I was airborne within a millisecond. I surprised myself a little but leaping across the table and grappling Cam to the ground was the most efficient way to express my umbrage with his behavior. Or at least that's how I chose to look at it as pint glasses and beer crashed to the floor in amber sheets. Cam and I met with a thud in the spreading mess. Annika screamed – or at least screamed at us.

Cam batted at me with one fist while playing keep-away from me with the other, then hitting me with it when convenient. The phone fist hurt more. I tried to catch this barrage with anything other than my head and shoulders and was momentarily able to suspend Cam's forearm in my armpit. I twisted around as best I could and pried his fingers. I was too close for him to land anything more harmful than a shiatsu massage – albeit a bad one. An elbow thudded into my ribs. I could take a couple more but that would be it. I rolled to my left and took his arm with me. It was impossible to break Cam's clench on the phone by more than a single finger so I improvised and sank my teeth into his wrist.

"Motherfucker!" he yelped as he dropped the phone into the puddle of beer. "You bit me?"

I snatched the phone and lurched up from my knees. I slipped on the beer but caught myself on a chair just long enough to see that Annika was staring at me. I couldn't tell if she was disgusted or concerned. Either way, she was not impressed. I was going to say something, I didn't know what but before I could...

"He bit me!" Cam yelled like a schoolyard tattle-tale. He clasped his wrist in his hand and jabbed the air at me with it. I straightened myself as best I could and limped out the door as the woodpecker held it open for me.

My teeth felt like I'd used them as a can opener. I wiped my mouth with the back of my hand and a smear of blood caught my eye. In all the excitement, I must have split my lip but I didn't recall taking a punch to the face. Then I realized it wasn't my blood. It was Cam's.

Great, I thought, now Annika thinks I'm vampire. And a Wookiee.

If the management culture of campus cops was the same as it was in my day, it would take about 15 minutes before they started combing the commons for a hirsute, 40-year-old male sanguivore, soaked in beer and brandishing a stolen mobile phone. I could just make it to Jude at the theater and get the Mini in time and maybe before I was due for a parking ticket. But why be greedy? I had the phone and more ledes than West Yorkshire as my old editor used to say. I just needed to rescue Jude from the youth-corrupting influence of Buntel Eriksson, transcribe some quotes and say my glory was I had such friends.

18.
Intermission

Unlike the grizzled old movie hams who predictably kvetch "I'm too old for this shit," at 40-something, I'm not. I'm just not good at anything overly physical. Fortunately, I seldom need be. This accounts for my relative longevity in the trade, or what's left of it. After all, I've still got my head.

It's not that I abhor violence, I just prefer to save my dwindling energies for going through the motions of love and other futilities. It's not that "I'm a lover, not a fighter," so much as I'm a writer, not a reporter. It's a different gig. More mammoth than mastodon, woolier but likewise slated for extinction.

That said, I understand the compulsion to be on one's beat. There's a locus of control that comes from having parameters within which to operate. Only my current beat, the freak beat, evolved into something wholly sinister. It was a pain in the ass. And neck and ribs. And pride.

I hobbled back to the screening room. Either Cam's punches were finally setting in or the pints were wearing off. I took the wheelchair ramp up to the door. Even though it was a longer walk, the sight of even five little steps made me weak in the knees.

Inside, the film archive was quiet and still. Futurist posters hung on the walls of the shallow room while the muffled soundtrack of the Plastic Spy hummed through the auditorium doors. No one was there, not even the student usher whose elective units depended on it.

I leaned into one of the auditorium doors, easing in so as not to disturb the screening or the bruise pooling beneath my shoulder. The light touch gained me nothing.

Den Plastspion was about halfway done – Sven Gerhardt was about to discover that the man he was assigned to spy on is – drumroll – Sven Gerhardt, himself. Bureaucratic snafu or Kafkaesque headtrip? The jury's out (smoking Gauloises). That's the best part of the film. After that, it rapidly goes downhill as he starts filing "reports" on his exploits. These entail little more than going to coffeehouses and writing down the fact that he'd been there, occasionally bedding a femme fatale and killing a supervillain in the most arbitrary of circumstances. Dream job. But boring cinema. Apparently, everyone else in class felt the same. The screening room was empty – no one was there. Including Jude.

Sonofabitch.

"Jude!" I yelled. Mine was just another voice in a chorus of improvised Swedish blather.

I scanned the seats to make sure Jude wasn't nested out of view. I didn't find him but the student usher resurrected, sprawled across a couple seats in the back row. The subtitles reflected in backwards gibberish off his glasses as if they were the projected contents of his mind.

"Wake up," I hissed from the head of the row. Why was I whispering? "Wake up!" I shouted.

The usher rolled his lazy head in my direction and moaned, "What the fuck, man?"

"Where's that kid that was here?"

"What kid?"

"What do you mean? He was your only customer."

"Oh, the kid. Hey, I'm not a babysitter, man," he said and laughed until he coughed. He was stoned. "A woman picked him up."

"A woman? Who?"

"I don't know, an older woman," he said, then added like some sort of bullshit connoisseur. "More cougar than MILF, groomed but not fussy. Ash blonde, dark eyes... Uh, *het...?*"

He was looking over my shoulder. I whipped around – no one was there apart from Swedish film star Rifka Benco on the big screen, whom he described down to the red lettering printed on her shirt that read "het."

Fucking stoners.

"She wasn't Rifka Benco."

He sat up, gave me the once-over. I was still a bloody mess.

"What the hell happened to you?" he asked.

"Smoked too much pot," I said.

He considered this, then bolted to his feet. "Oh, shit. What if the kid was kidnapped? That makes me an accessory!" he said. Then pacing, "I got priors, man, I can't handle that kind of shit!"

"Do you know when she got him?"

He didn't. I turned to the screen.

"What reel are we on?" Of all the trivial knowledge I'd amassed over the years, it never occurred to me that knowing the plot points of a Buntel Eriksson film would one day prove useful.

The usher blinked. He had no idea what I was talking about. Of course, no reels – everything was digital now.

"Which cut is this?" I demanded. "Swedish or the American theatrical release?"

147

"Swedish," he said with mild derision, as if "there were no other." Longer by an hour, the Swede version made even less sense than the American cut but every neckbeard worth his fedora thought it superior.

On screen, Benco was about to do the famous "handjob" scene, which wasn't a handjob at all but rather her clandestine reloading the titular character's gun, which she slides into Gerhardt's lap under the table at a dinner party table as our hero performs a card trick to a rapt rogues' gallery of guests. It's classic Eriksson misdirection: Is he distracting them from her, or is she distracting them from – BANG! The gag pays off precisely at minute one-hundred and fifty-four when the Plastic Spy blows away the dreaded Haakon the Noogin from across the table. Close up on his bloody monocle, which has landed on the ace of spades (where else?). Two-and-a-half hours and change.

Jude and his newfound chaperone had quite a jump on me. A couple hours in any direction from Lumaville and one could be halfway to Nevada, at SFO, in the Emerald Triangle or five miles out to sea. Then I realized this wasn't going to be a chase. This was to be a transaction. I had two phones in my coat pockets and I knew which one would they would ring.

* * *

I darted across the boulevard. I didn't have Cam's finesse with traffic and was nearly clipped by a girl on an electric scooter. I did a three-sixty in the middle of the street in the wake of her silent whoosh. No sign of Jude. My sides were beginning to ache and I needed to sit down. I figured I could at least make it up the block to the campus cafe and maybe be able to fall in the general direction of the Mini when the time came – that is, if I hadn't already died from internal bleeding.

At the cafe, I flopped into the first seat I could find, right by the entryway along the railing. It was a bench and I hung my arms out wide along the rail so as not to touch my ribs. None were broken so far as I could tell, but part of me thought it might've been better if they were somehow, as if they were still contorting under Cam's blows but ached worse because they had yet to give. That said, the pain in my gut hurt worse though I didn't recall Cam landing any ab jabs, not that, truth be told, I had any abs to jab. No, it was the white-hot worry for Jude. It seared against the haphazard sutures of an old wound. I had failed again. I had failed another kid. I cornered the market on letting down the youth of America – 220 feet down last time. Who knows where in the world, or indeed, worlds, he had been taken.

I tried to think it through: If Jude were kidnapped by a past–her–prime Rifka Benco lookalike he would've put up a fight and made enough ruckus for the stoned usher to at least wake up if not act by pulling a fire alarm or something. To wit, it must've been someone Jude knew and if not someone he trusted, then perhaps someone to whom he could be convinced he owed a karmic debt. Like an older woman whose mobile phone he had stolen on a SMART train. In which case this Dr. Ashe was the candidate.

And I had her precious. To think that I had an instrument of interdimensional travel in my pocket. I could barely afford the data plan on my own phone let alone one with a version of *The Knights of Skeldaria* that opened wormholes. Clearly, this was a costly proposition for Dr. Ash. My question was how did she know where Jude was, since finding an American preadolescent at a Buntel Erickson screening had more odds against it than could be accounted for by even the penultimate integer.

A mustachioed busser ambled by with a tub overflowing with used cappuccino cups.

"We don't do tableservice, mate," he said. "You have to order inside."

His mustache boasted enough wax to be a pair of birthday candles grafted to his smug mug. He'd do well to never ask me for a light.

I made an empty harrumph and leaned like I might get up but went right back down on my ass. It was the pain in my side and the pain of the obvious, all at once, that grounded me.

It was Cam who tipped Ashe about the kid. I stupidly bigmouthed the factoid and he put the heel on her to get him. To have leverage. On me. That's why he gave up her phone so easily. He already had a plan in motion.

A phone rang. I patted my pocket but it was in vain. A student a few tables down answered his phone, "Where are you?" to which the young woman brushing past the entrance, her own phone pressed against a ruddy cheek, answered, "I'm here, where are you?" The dude's head popped up like a periscope and swiveled until their eyes met and smiles of mock exasperation bloomed between them.

That's when it occurred to me that the stolen uber-phone in my pocket probably wasn't the only one of its ilk. After all, what good is a single phone? Even Alexander Graham Bell needed a pal. There must be at least another phone with the same unlocked Easter Egg and overheating internal electronics, or more. Maybe the whole shebang worked on some kind of network distributed across many-worlds – like "reach out and touch someone" and "E.T. phone home" all at once.

* * *

I used the wiper-blade to grab the parking ticket off the Mini's windshield and slapped it in the glove box with the rest. I put the Mini in gear and rolled by every place I knew was familiar to Jude.

The spider web of police tape at Gemelli Brothers had already been replaced with an "Under New Management" sign. That was fast, even for downtown Lumaville, which was always in the midst of retail roulette. I remembered I still hadn't paid for the coat but I was loathe to mention it lest Detective Shane come and claim it as evidence. The X on the breast pocket had faded into a vague white smudge so I looked less like modern art and more like a regular slob. Jude wasn't there. Nor was he at the Big Box store. I avoided the cop shop and drove homeward. I needed to get cleaned up before doing anymore footwork. I also had half a hope Jude would be there as he was the last time he pulled a Houdini.

In my building, I lurched up the stairs and down the hall. My door was slightly ajar – a relief to see. I pushed it open with the tips of my fingers and quietly queried "Jude?" as if checking on a sleeping baby or gingerly approaching a junkyard dog. It was neither kid nor canine that greeted me inside.

As a card-carrying member of Gen X, I have an innate appreciation for most creations of the 80s, with the exception of the Glock 19. The preferred pistol of law-enforcement, it holds 15 rounds and weighs only 30 ounces when fully-loaded. Its slim profile makes it a favorite with plainclothes officers as it doesn't upset the tailored silhouette of a jacket. In fact, had she not pointed it at my face, I wouldn't have known Detective Shane packed one. She shook her head as she holstered it inside her coat.

"Fire your cleaning service?" She said.

I scanned the room. The place had been tossed. Papers littered the floor, drawers were pulled from their slides and emptied. Not even my infernal couch was spared. It looked like the college fencing team used it for an anger management exercise.

"Got a warrant?" I asked.

"Door was open," she said, "Wide open."

"Your handy work, I presume?" I gestured to the new interior decorating.

"Like this when I got here," she said. "Mostly."

I started gathering papers from the floor but I was too sore, so instead I rolled onto Edward Scissor Couch.

"I don't know what kind of shit you're in but you look like shit, your place looks like shit and your coffee sure as hell tastes like shit," she said. "But all that's your problem. My problem is that The Artful Dodger gave me the slip and you haven't been straight about who he is and where he's been. Contributing to the delinquency of a minor, housing a runaway, obstruction, generally being a dick. Shall I go on?"

"Let me get us some proper cups of coffee and I'll explain everything."

"It's already on its way."

On cue, an arch-looking barista from downstairs tapped on the door with the two mugs looped through her grainy fingers. In her other hand was a brimming press–pot.

"Pair of aces," the barista said as she put the kit down atop my piano. Detective Shane paid, tipped well. The barista strode through the wreckage of my apartment like an icebreaker, cash in hand. She left the door open, which I closed after sloshing through what was once a neatly stacked pile of unfinished manuscripts.

"So...?" said Shane.

"Okay. But you're not going to believe me. At least not at first," I preambled.

"Didn't expect to believe you at all," she said.

I found her lack of faith alluring. I sat back on the shredded couch. Shane stood.

"To begin with, we accept that Lumaville is a city of anomalous phenomena, right?"

"You've been on the freak beat too long, Dade."

"Sure, but I wager you have too."

"Try me," she said.

I spit it out.

"The kid is from a parallel universe, an alternate reality, brought here by a cracked app on a stolen mobile phone made by Cameron Block. Who wants it back."

Shane took a long pull on her coffee and finally said, "I should've gotten something stronger."

"Now that's a notion by which I can abide. Let me take you out for a drink."

"I meant espresso. You flirting with me?" she squinted.

"Is it working?"

"No," she said.

Shane sighed and shook her head.

"Ever tell you how we closed the Miss Lumaville case?"

"Dead girl in the river. Big story for us."

"Hmm," Shane muttered as she took a sip. "We had trouble identifying the body at first. There was the natural deterioration, of course, but there she was – white dress hanging on her bony little shoulders, no tits to speak of, the pink 'Ms. Lumaville' sash tight around her neck. She had the tiara pinned in her hair still. And back at the morgue we discovered what else she had."

I was coming up blank and Shane knew it.

"A penis, Dade," said Shane. "She had a penis."

"She was a boy?"

"Yep. Or there was a deceased teenage male who acquired her clothes then got himself asphyxiated and dumped in the Lumaville River," she said. "We had a real puzzle until the parents came to identify the body."

"And?"

"They said it was her," said Shane with a shrug. "So we left it at that. But that's when I learned a little something about Lumaville, Dade. What we choose to call 'reality' here is a choice."

I mulled this a second and decided it begged for a follow up question.

"So, what reality *did* you choose, Shane?"

"To keep my eyes open and mouth shut until I know the score," she said. "Listen, you're finally seeing Lumaville for what it is – and you're right, it is a city of 'anomalous phenomena.' But if you want to make it here – and by that I mean not end up in the river in a debutante dress – you might consider doing the same."

Detective Shane knelt to some toppled books on the floor. Among them she plucked the photo of Annika that used to be on the piano. "He has her eyes," she said.

19.
Word of the Day

Meaninglessness. This word has long bothered me. It's essentially a four-letter word with three suffixes. A Mini Cooper pulling a trio of trailers – uphill. It's an ungainly, stupid way to build a word. Why didn't anyone call the Germans when the crossword clue "Fifteen letter word for abject existential horror" came up? Surely any Kraut worth their *Fahrvergnügen* could do better than "meaninglessness." Consider their *Bedeutungslosigkeit*, a word that's practically a philosophy in itself, with its own parking space. Or the Japanese: *muimi*, which makes you want to pet it...or spank it. Perhaps in some other universe, like Jude's, where all the coulda, shoulda, wouldas occurred the way they coulda, shoulda, woulda, there's a better word for meaninglessness. A word that's piquant and percussive and most likely followed by "you."

They would probably mess it up too.

Fuckinglessness. That old familiar feeling.

The cemetery was on the north end of town on Magnolia avenue. It's the centerpiece of what we called Death Row – the adjacent Catholic cemetery is on its east, a Jewish cemetery is sandwiched in between, and there's a pet cemetery on the northern end. The plots on my itinerary, however, had a certain pedigree – all of the city's founders, dating back to the 1850s were interned here, all WASPs, tellingly self-segregated, even in death, from the Catholics, Jews and dogs.

I rolled up the narrow driveway, through the stone and wrought-iron arch and along the pitted asphalt roadway. Cypress Hill was a web of narrow avenues, navigable by Model A's and Mini Coopers. 1K's plot also offered drive-thru service but I parked instead and wove through the obelisks, weeping angels and family mausoleums with more square footage than my apartment. It was a wedged-shaped marker those in burying business called a "pillow top" since its dimensions were approximately those of a cushion suitable for resting one's dead head.

The stone was larger than I remembered and 1K's name was carved, all caps, in a blocky serifed font just like the one next to it and the one next to that. It reminded me that we once called abutting newspaper headlines "tombstones." 1K's, however, was a bit of false advertising. It had a slab of granite and the faded remains of artificial flowers but no body. It was technically a cenotaph, merely a monument, since 1K's leap from the Golden Gate Bridge came with a complimentary burial at sea. I wasn't sure why his parents sprung for the real estate but it was worth the view – rolling hills quilted with vineyards and dotted by the occasional black sheep.

I laid my head on the pillow and hoped for twenty centuries of stony sleep as I slipped the last half–moon of Lorazapam under my tongue.

In the 80s, my family lived in a condo complex across the street and next to the local mortuary that had sprouted like a mushroom within this ecosystem of death. My kid brother and I would play along the banks of the gully that separated the complex from the parking lot, staging mock funerals for beheaded *Star Wars* figures we drenched in the viscera of single-serve ketchup packets. It was our Tom and Huck familiarity with the land of the dead that enabled me to sneak out of 1K's funeral five years ago. With a woosh of my coat, I disappeared behind a slab of sandstone carved with script and the biblical equivalent of clip art and emerged a block later on Keokuk Street en route to the bar. This is how I met Crysta the barista, though it took four more years for the mutual desperation to overflow our thimble-sized self respect.

I closed my eyes and contemplated the fuckinglessness of my life. I thought about what happens when you die and decided what happens when you *don't* is probably worse. I thought about 1K and of Jude and about half a dozen other defining failures – Annika, the mentally disabled kid at the bus stop, old Mac and President Dewey, terminations of every stripe, my dying trade, my precious car...

With its white top and red body, finding my Mini in a parking lot, no matter how vast, is usually a cinch. In a sea of sedans and SUVs, the Mini stands out like a pimple. But this was a different sort of situation. The parking lot was infinite. And every car in it was a Mini Cooper with a white top and red body. They were all my car. And each one had a parking ticket.

I approached one, not the closest one, that would be too obvious, but one near it. I looked in the window – same to-go coffee cup mouldering in the console, same papers I've meant to file for six months, same collection of tickets accruing penalties and interest, same wrappers and matchbooks, same discarded burrito foil and stray Portage brand reporter's notebooks. Every car was a clone of the other with the same detritus of the same wretchedly-lived life. I tried my key in the door. It worked – why wouldn't it? I got in and pulled the door closed. Same stale reek of a random cigarette I smoked inside the car weeks ago, breaking my own rules for no reason other than I was bored. Same hole in the floor mat worn by the heel of my Beatle boot, ground to a wedge staggering the streets of Lumaville.

As I put the key in the ignition, I heard a pounding, like the flabby thump of a kick drum in need of tightening. It was coming from the next Mini over. Inside was Annika, in her lab coat, black curls flying as she beat the passenger side window with the soft bottoms of her fists.

"Fergus," she yelled, fogging the window as her fists stamped a dozen baby footprints. "That's the wrong car!"

Oh shit. I pulled the latch but it didn't give. The door was locked. I flicked the toggle switch in the dash – nothing. I was locked in. I tried the other door. Ditto.

Annika kept yelling, "You're in the wrong car!" But she wasn't the only one. Through my passenger window I could see in the adjacent Mini yet another Annika stretching over the driver's seat and drumming the window with her fists. She too insisted that I was in the wrong car. If I could only get out, I thought, I might be able to pull off the ultimate threesome. But then another Annika began screaming at me from the car in back of mine. And yet another from in front. There were thousands of cars and thousands of Annikas all pleading "Fergus! You're in the wrong car! Fergus! You're in the wrong car!"

Some of the more enterprising Annikas punctuated their refrain by beeping their respective car horns. The voices began to synchronize, organize, until a booming single voice began to emerge, unified in a single command: "Fucking wake up!"

I came to with a start. Annika hovered above me, haloed by the setting sun. She wasn't quite angelic, in fact, she looked downright bitchy but that's what I liked about her. It was the way she did her eyebrows, arched such that she looked like she was always about to ask "What the fuck is wrong with you?" Which is precisely what she said next.

"I'm taking a nap."

"It took me five minutes to wake you up," she said. "It was like you were in a coma."

"How did you find me?"

"Where else would you be? You come here every year on this day."

"Do I?" I had no idea what day it was.

"And you changed your phone number," she said. I didn't – I had to change providers due to a disagreement over the bill (I didn't feel like paying it).

"So, you stalked me?"

"Don't flatter yourself," she said.

"I had a dream that we were about to do it with your clone," I said.

"Is that why you were screaming?" she said. "Sorry to ruin your Double Mint commercial."

"We could do it right here," I offered.

"First off, no. Second off, on your intern's grave?"

I was going to make a joke about 1K being "fucked over" again but refrained. And that, my friend, is called "maturity."

I gathered myself and sat upright. The half slug of Lorazepam was still doing its job. I leaned on Annika's shoulder, which she yielded to me as I buried my face in her knit scarf. She sighed.

"You were right."

I had no idea what I was right about so I played like I knew so I wouldn't be wrong.

"Cameron is evil," she said. "He told me about Ashe and the app, 'The Knights of Skeldaria,' what they've been working on. What they've already done. It's bad. It's all very bad."

"How far are you in it?"

"Not much – worked on some pieces but I was in the dark. With Ashe on the outs, he offered me the keys to the kingdom if I'd join him."

"But?"

"I'm at my ex's dead intern's grave instead," she said. "So..."

"It's not really a grave. It's a cenotaph on account of they never found the body."

"I get it. Surfaces can be deceiving," she said.

She straightened the collar of my coat, steadied me. "Why? Why do you come here?"

"Habit," I said off-handed.

Then she gathered my lapels in her fists with that mock anger women use to show they care. "It's not your fault, Fergus, you know that, right? It's not your fault."

I'd heard that before and I knew it was true. Sure. In the years after a tragedy, one collects a lot of platitudes. You accept them, file them, never look at them again. But what Annika said next I'd never heard before. I suspect the sheer novelty of it – its truth, its consideration, the appreciation of history as happenstance, as collusion of chemistry and opportunity, an accident of fate – is why I ended up soaking her scarf with half a decade's dishevelled tide.

"It's not his fault either," she said.

20.
Murderer's Thumb

Annika adjusted the driver's seat, mirrors and radio, then turned the key. The Mini lit up, including the gas light, which caused my ex to sigh.

"Drunk?"

"Lorazepam," I said. "I but I can fix it with two cups of coffee."

Annika peeled onto the avenue and zipped up toward town. She drove the Mini better than I did and always had. She had a talent with machines, anything mechanical, whereas my facility ended with a corkscrew. All the more reason for her to drive.

"First off, I believe you," she said.

"Even if you don't, it's nice to hear you say it," I said as I eased the seat back. "Sometimes, I don't even believe me but what's the worst that can happen?"

"You end up trapped in a parallel universe living out a hollow simulacra of your life."

Simulacra. I was there when Annika learned the word. It was one of her buzzwords in the 90s, like "postmodernism," "deconstruction" and "student loan default." What she didn't know was that I already was living out a hollow simulacra of my life. Or at least the life I thought I'd have, one I once thought would have her in it.

"The reason I believe you is because I know it's worked before," she said. "I know that Dr. Ashe, at least, has traveled between two iterations."

Another buzz word. "Iterations?"

"Of probability. Of all possible outcomes – other universes. And that's how your boy got himself stuck here."

She plucked an unfiltered cigarette from the top pocket of her jacket and punched the Mini's cigarette lighter.

"I don't smoke in the car," I said.

She glared at me for a couple of long seconds before the lighter popped out and she lit her smoke.

"Your boy must have figured out how to hack the app – at the very least a password – on Ashe's phone," she said. The lids to her brown eyes lifted a moment then dropped back into shrewd slits. "How old is he?"

"I don't know – eleven? Pre-tween, if that's a word."

She did some quiet math in her head.

"Why do you think he came to you, Fergus?"

"His prefrontal cortex isn't developed enough to make rational decisions."

She squinted.

"You said it about me once."

"I was right," she said, exhaling smoke. "I'm still right."

"What's odd is that he knew my name. My name–name, not my byline," I said. "He pulled it out of his hat when he thought I was going to ditch him at the police station."

Annika sucked in her cheeks and nodded. Something was eating at her but she wouldn't let on.

"He must be scared," she said. "And someone must really miss him."

"Who?"

"His parents. Duh."

"Duh," I echoed. Until now, the thought hadn't occurred

to me. Jude had arrived in my life fully formed and without a backstory, like one of those mushrooms that suddenly appear on the edges of people's lawns after a storm.

"Well, good thing he has us smarty–pants grownups on the job," she said.

Annika stopped the car. And waited.

"Well?"

She had a way of looking at me like I was the stupidest motherfucker in the world.

"Get your coffee, man. And one for me."

We were already idling in front of the cafe.

* * *

Annika parked us on the crest of B Street by the water tower. The town below looked like a miniature train set – a grid of twinkling lights, divided by the Lumaville River and the commuter rail tracks that paralleled it until the river pitched thirty degrees west.

Teenagers used the discrete strip of parking lot to have sex in their cars. Used condoms littered the gutter like the carcasses of balloon animals – parts of a poodle, a cobra, possibly a sea anemone.

"You know," I began but Annika shushed me.

"I'm thinking," she said. She took a long sip of her coffee but made no mention of how I fixed it up for her – two percent lowfat milk, half a packet of raw sugar.

"Can I see it?" Annika asked as she looked over the lid.

I looked at my lap just long enough for her to get the joke I was pretending I was not making.

"The phone."

I held it out for her. She grabbed it but I didn't let go at first.

"Be careful," I said.

"I know what I'm doing," she said as she glided a clubbed thumb over the glass face of the phone. There was a time when she was self-conscious about it, of her truncated digit that seemed to end a quarter-inch prematurely and finished with a short, wide nail. To the untrained eye, it looked like it was bitten off above the joint, like a world class nail-biter. But, as Annika routinely explained to the curious and rude, was actually "brachydactyly type D." I took her word for it, though a palm reader we once saw together referred to it as her "murderer's thumb."

Annika's eyes reflected the aquamarine splash screen of *The Knights of Skeldaria* app.

"Why so confident you're not going to send us into another dimension?"

"Because I wrote it."

"You wrote 'The Knights of Skeldaria?'" I said.

"I wrote the code in the Easter Egg," she said. Her eyes brightened. "And there it is," she said and turned to me. "My Easter Egg. Lord knows how he cracked it. The password is impossible. Personal."

"Why in the world would you put it in 'The Knights of Skeldaria?'" I asked.

"Ubiquity. If you knew how to activate it, you could effectively turn any device with the app on it into a means of traveling through the multiverse. We only infected two, however. One for Dr. Ashe and one for Cameron. That's all we needed for our research."

"One to call. And one to answer."

"Not exactly, but that'll pass as a layman's analogy," Annika said. I was apparently the layman. She took another sip of her coffee and asked, "What's the boy's name?"

"Jude."

"Always liked that name."

"It's a Beatle name. If he was a girl he could be Sadie or Lucy," I said.

Annika nodded absently, sipped, then snapped back to business.

"To send Jude back, we need to know precisely when he arrived here. That'll allow me to basically reverse-engineer where he came from."

"It's not on the phone?"

She held the phone in her hand like a model in an infomercial.

"No, this phone, this app, is calibrated to another time and place entirely. The place he's from, his timeline, his universe. It's like when you fly from coast to coast but don't adjust your watch."

Another layman's analogy, but I got it.

"Unless we can think of another way to get his arrival time, he's stuck here."

Wherever he is, I thought to myself.

I pressed my face against the cool glass of the passenger window. A deep sigh fogged it up and I traced a finger through it, making a figure eight. I had a headache. Or maybe it was heartache. I mean, who was this woman sitting next me, smoking in my car, nattering away about mobile phones, hacking the multiverse, Easter Eggs and who knows what else? She was not the woman I dated in various fits of failed domesticity every seven years or so since college. She had evolved into someone else, something far more slithery than a moon-eyed Swede with the dark locks and weird thumb.

"Cameron is obsessed," Annika said, eyes out the window. "When you showed up with the phone and your story about the kid, I knew he was going to lose his shit."

"Why?"

"Because he hadn't gone that far yet," she said. "But Ashe

165

did. Weeks ago. She disappeared with the prototype. Or, more likely, the prototype disappeared with her. Cameron was too scared to try it himself. He only experimented with objects. Like when he opened a mini wormhole to age wine through relativity," she added with a snort. "It was really good."

My face became very hot and I clenched my teeth so hard I would have cracked a molar had I not suddenly barked, "You people ever stop to think about what you were doing? From an ethical standpoint? Did you ever think you might break the universe?"

Annika reeled back, appalled. The lid plastic popped off her coffee from gripping the cup so tightly.

"I'm not going to let the man who stole his pseudonym from a Buntel Eriksson film lecture me on ethics," she spat back.

"First off, sister, it's a byline. Second off, Buntel Eriksson is probably the greatest Swedish filmmaker there ever was —"

"Unless you're Swedish."

"You're American."

"Tell that to my passport."

"Which one? You got two," I said, then added, for kicks, "Like a criminal."

"I'm the criminal? I'm the fucking criminal?" She turned the ignition. Nothing happened. She tried again and the Mini sputtered to life.

"We need gas," I said. "Or we're taking the train."

"No shit," she sighed.

Annika pointed the Mini down B Street and we rolled toward town, passing the handsome Queen Anne victorians and craftsman-style homes that lined the street. She chewed her lip instead of talking to me. When we pulled into the fluorescent glare of a gas station she passed me a twenty.

She knew I didn't have any gas money.

I told the sad-eyed man behind the counter to put it all on Six as if I was playing roulette. He carefully closed the book he was reading – "Become a Tax Preparer" – and opened the till. I watched the video monitor on the opposing wall. On it was a sticker that read "Notice: This Area is Under 24-Hour Video Surveillance." Onscreen was a grainy Annika using the Mini's rearview mirror to put on lipstick.

"Receipt?" the man asked. I shook my head and he shook his back.

I pumped the gas. Eventually, Annika rolled down the driver-side window and climbed out of the seat to harangue me over the roof of the car.

"And we did think about the ethics," Annika said. She had a habit of continuing conversations in her head. "Please note how Ashe was her own Guinea pig."

She put a cigarette on her lip but thought better than to light it.

"The kind of ethics to make Dr. Jekyll proud," I retorted.

"Did you get a receipt?" she asked.

Shit.

I reached into my breast pocket and fished around my reporter's notebook for something that could pass. I pulled out a wadded up ball of tea-colored tissue and carefully opened it.

It was Mac's clip.

"I interviewed a hundred year-old guy who was also a Guinea pig. For this guy..."

I handed Annika the clip. She gasped.

Annika gasped. "That's her. That's Professor Ashe," she said.

I looked at the inky halftone that crested the clip.

"That's a dude," I said, poking a finger at the bespectacled, long–faced man in the photo.

"Behind him," she said, "Look."

I hadn't noticed before but, indeed, there was a lanky woman in profile standing to the right of the man. I looked at the cutline but Mac had ripped the page such that any names were lost in the tear.

"She looks the same," said Annika.

"How's that even possible?"

"She must be jumping around. Time and space are meaningless to her. It could be last century or last week to her. Or even next week."

I rolled the clip up and dropped it back in my pocket.

"The man who wrote this was a hundred years old. He thought there was a President Dewey. Why did he end up here? What the hell is going on?"

Annika shook her head. A couple of curls fell in front of her eyes, then parted when she tipped the last sip of coffee between her lips.

"Good coffee," she said because she had nothing else to say.

I leaned toward her.

"I need to tell you something," I said.

"Don't even try..."

"I don't know where Jude is."

She closed her eyes and sat silently for a moment, like she was in a mini–trance. Her eyes flashed opened behind her chunky glasses.

"That we can fix. But there's a bigger problem. We call it the Quantum Deadline."

21.
The Short Goodbye

Of all the crocks of shit that Annika threw at me that past few days (nay, years, I realized) the notion of a "quantum deadline" was by far the most annoying. Not least of which because it borrowed one of the few sacred words remaining in my trade – deadline. And also because she had developed an irritating taste for jargon. Sometimes she sounded like she learned English from business books and TED Talks. Sometimes, it didn't sound like English at all but rather some psycholinguistic form of subterfuge meant to beguile or alienate, or trick the natives. Cameron Block was good at it and now so was Annika. She had become a liar.

"What?" she sighed, then turned the ignition.

"Quantum deadline sounds like the shitty marketing the Millennial marketeers at my blog gig cook up: We're on Quantum Deadline – Publishing at the Speed of News," I said. Annika was not impressed, with my gag or my gig.

"It's serious," she said as she whipped the Mini in a backward semicircle with nary a glance in the mirrors. Annika had enough of the view. She was restless like that, always needed fresh stimuli. Like most kids who had their genius misdiagnosed as A.D.D. back in the 90s, she needed to keep feeding the machine lest it start taking itself apart from boredom.

"A quantum deadline defines the time in which a portal to another universe can remain open," she said. "That's why we have to get Jude back as soon as possible. Before his time runs out."

Annika reached into her pocket and came back with a pack of cigarettes, a credit card, a lipstick and a compact mirror. Getting ready for a night out? Nope. She put everything back but the compact, which she opened and held to my wrist. Its dusty surface reflected the watch she gave me back in the halcyon days of Christmas Past.

"Hold this. Look in the reflection," she said. "What time would be the same on both your watch and the mirror?"

I thought about it. If it were 3 p.m. it would look like 9 p.m. in the reflection. Hmm. I was taking too long to answer her.

"Midnight. And noon. When the little and big hands are both on the twelve," she said, then added, "That came out more patronizing than I meant."

"Go on."

"And I'm sorry.

"No, I mean – are you saying Jude came in at noon and has to be out by midnight? Because then he's fucked."

"No. It's an analogy. The twelve on your watch and the twelve in the mirror represent the two parallel points where the individual universes connect – when they align. And it's ephemeral. These two points represent the door. One way in," she put a hand at the top of the steering wheel. "One way out." She traced a path around the steering wheel until her hands met at the top. "And if you miss it, you can't get back."

"So, what is it? A time, a place?"

"It's neither and it's both. It's a *probability* and when

the Easter Egg in the app is activated it finds the point of alignment and opens a door. Until it closes."

She snapped the compact shut and yanked it away. It took a few hairs on my wrist with it but I was too tired to complain about it.

"So how much time do we have?"

"I don't know," Annika said. "Each deadline is unique."

I fiddled with the glove box. I rarely sat in the passenger seat of my own car, unless I was planning on sleeping in it.

"Why do I feel like you're making me a 'limited time offer?'" I asked.

Annika finally cracked a window and blew out a lungful of credibility, then took a deep breath and got it all back.

"How long have you known?"

"Since you picked me up. Cameron sent you, didn't he?"

"Yes, but it's not like you think."

"I'm an optimist. Nothing is ever like I think. It's always way fucking worse. How did you know where to find me?"

"It's the anniversary of your intern's death, you go every year," she said.

I didn't realize it was 1K's deathday, if that's a word, but I was pleased to learn I had some consistency in my life.

"Cameron blackmailed Ashe into picking Jude up," she said. "Without Cam she can't get back. You see, she's from there..."

"Of course she is and so is Jude and so was old Mac the newspaperman," I said. "Is Cameron blackmailing you too? What's he got – pictures? Lurid selfies?"

"First off, fuck you. And second, off, you don't understand. Cameron goes back and forth – between the universes. He has an entire scam he's created, a duplicate world that he's intellectually stripmining, a place to beta test, a control, anything you could imagine doing in a parallel universe."

"He's fucking himself, isn't he?"

Annika laughed – snorted, really – which caused her to laugh more. As she recovered, I cupped my hand around hers, took the cigarette from between her fingers and had a drag. I remembered Annika always smoked strong cigarettes as I stifled a cough.

"And you're supposed to broker the deal with me to get the phone that allows him to do that," I said. "The phone for the kid."

She wasn't laughing anymore. Instead, she dipped her eyes and sighed hard. It was enough to fog the rose–tinted glasses with which I regarded our relationship.

"You don't understand..."

"...That you're quite a mercenary?"

Annika slapped the cigarette right out of my mouth. It flew into the windshield and exploded like fireworks over the dashboard. I patted them out as Annika pounded her fists on the steering wheel.

"I'm trying to make this right, goddamnit!" she screamed. I waited a beat for the tears but they didn't come. Instead, her eyes welled with white hot anger. "This is not what I signed up for but this is what happened. And I need you to help me fix it."

"So, Cameron has Jude?"

"I know he has him. I just don't know where. Or when. Or..."

"You just used two of the five W's, better slow down before you run out of interrogatives."

"I know the answers to the others. Including How and Why if you have to know," she said, "So spare me the interview tactics."

"I gotta cop buddy if you wanna upgrade to an interrogation," I said.

"You wouldn't."

"I might."

Annika lit another cigarette and squinted through the smoke at me to gauge my seriousness. I went as blank as I could. She and I had once watched the same documentary on micro–expressions, the tell–tale tics between our smiles and frowns but only Annika got good at it, which is why I had to quit playing poker with her.

"I like the tough guy act, Fergus. But, you gotta understand that we're on the same side. We're both here for Jude. I'll tell you – I only saw him for a moment but I recognized him. Never seen him before in my life but I recognized him. And I'm pretty sure he recognized me. That happened to you too. I know it. And we both know why we have to help him."

"I've been helping him. I'm just really bad at it," I said. "Besides, if we give up the phone for Jude, then he's stuck here."

"I know. But we're here. And we're all he's got."

"According to your science experiment, we're there too."

"No, we're not," she said. A grimness washed over her. "Trust me. You don't want to know."

Of course I did, but it wasn't the moment.

Finally, a tear arrived. Curiously, it rolled sideways from the corner of her eye and into the dark curls that framed the crest of her cheekbone. Annika always did have a strange center of emotional gravity.

"When did we become such horrible people?" she said, grandfathering me in.

"I suspect we've always been horrible people," I said. "But when you're long in the tooth the fangs blend in."

Annika looked at me, wistful and stricken. Then she squinted and said "What the fuck does that mean?" as she wiped snot on the back of her fist.

As we drove into town it occurred to me that I'd known her too long to tell her age. Maybe others saw the woman in her forties Annika purported to be but if anything had waned in her it was for all eyes but these eyes.

* * *

The coffee was beginning to do its job. It was a toss up which it would activate first, my brain or my colon. Brain won this time. I thought about what Jude had told me about stealing the phone from the old woman on the SMART train, about playing *The Knights of Skeldaria* and about activating the Easter Egg. I also thought about the job the coffee was doing and how the beer Annika ordered me while I was in the john would do it better. That said, I would have chosen any other joint in Lumaville to acquire said beer but Annika found parking in front of my usual place, so that was it.

"To do this right, I need to know the precise time that Jude entered our universe," Anika explained. "Then I can calibrate a trip back through the same portal that delivered him."

"What could go wrong?" I japed, but she kept serious.

"An infinite amount of things – literally. That's why we use the Penultimate Integer. We need to subtract one probability from an infinite amount of probabilities."

"There's more than one?"

"Yes, Fergus," Annika patronized, "That's why we call it a 'multiverse.' Otherwise, you end up in the wrong place and totally insane. You might not even notice it at first. Until something subtle, like the spinach eggs Benedict at the cafe, is suddenly gone and none of the waitstaff has any idea what you're talking about because in their universe it never existed. Then you're fucked."

"Or you're President Dewey," I said.

"Or you're President Dewey," she echoed. "Because, yes, 'Dewey Wins' somewhere. Nice reference."

"Thanks."

"That's why we have the app to do it. The versions of The Knights of Skeldaria that have the Easter Egg have the Penultimate Integer. Guarantees you get back to the same place you came from. But to do that, we need to know the precise time the portal opened. The precise time Jude arrived."

"Wouldn't there be a record on the phone?" I asked as I reached for it in my pocket. I didn't take it out – I just wanted to make sure it was still there.

"No, she said, it's like traveling time zones. If you go from New York to L.A. your watch is on New York time still – ditto with his phone."

The door to the bar whooshed open and with it came a rush of chilly air and the specter of Edwin, wrapped in a scarf that was longer than his collective word count. He saluted me boy scout style when our eyes briefly met and took a seat at the bar. I had no idea what utility Adriane the Editrix got out of him besides a means of punishing herself for past omissions or getting him to write shit stories like the one about SMART train surveillance cameras watching paint dry on murals.

"Surveillance cameras," I said. "They just installed surveillance cameras on the SMART train. They probably have a time code."

Annika straightened in the booth that had otherwise enveloped her.

"Right! And you said that Jude had stolen the phone and activated the app on the train – his train. But he got off on ours. Holy shit. The timecode on the surveillance video, of course – can we get it?" she asked.

I nodded: "If they've got a community relations person or

some kind of publicist it would make it a hell of a lot easier. I'll pitch some bogus story, get myself into the channels. I'll need your laptop."

"Yours," Annika said, then added apropos of nothing, "Also, the barmaid is a skank."

I hushed her, instinctively.

"Ah, shit. You didn't tell her that did you?"

"She's been giving me side–eye ever since you sat down. She's doing it agin. And where the hell are the beers I ordered anyway?"

As if summoned, Crysta beelined toward us clutching two brews. She all but dropped my beer onto the imitation woodgrain table, though she probably would've preferred my lap. She stood such that she eclipsed Annika.

"Hey, Dade," Crysta said as she moved to light the candle between us.

Annika mouthed "Dade?" at me and rolled her eyes. She never liked the byline and nicknames derived from it she found all the more fatuous.

"Crysta," I said.

In her hand was a stove lighter. She pulled the trigger at me and a flame danced at the end of it. If she were a cartoon, it would've been a pistol that emitted a flag that read "Bang!"

She dipped her weapon into the mason jar on the table and lit the tea candle inside.

"There," she said. "More romantic."

Crysta hovered, silent, just a tick long enough for us all to become uncomfortable.

"Uh, thanks," I said.

"You're welcome," she said, her words overlapping mine. Then she walked away, torn denim hips swaying.

Annika stared at me pie–eyed, mouth agape, for a moment. Then she giggled.

"Blow a kiss, 'Dade,'" she said with a shit–eating grin.

"Why?"

"'Cuz you're kissing that ass goodbye," she laughed.

* * *

I opened Annika's laptop. I found the bar's wifi signal (Take My Wifi, Please) and entered the password she had shared with me and was surely soon to change. "A".

Finding out who runs security at a public transit agency is easy enough but trying to connect with them is another matter entirely. After SMART raised the ire of hackers by killing wifi and cell phone connectivity in its stations, threats were made, accounts hacked and private information smeared all over the Internet like peanut butter. Consequently, the site was scrubbed of anything identifying – or useful. Fair enough, but it made "media inquiries" a nightmare. That was my angle – ye olde media inquiry – it's always my angle. About twenty pages deep, I found a phone number for its PR office, but no email.

I borrowed Annika's phone and a smoke. I took a quick hit off the candle and ducked outside to exhale and make my call.

The publicist answered on the third ring and I breathlessly made my case.

"Who do you write for again?" the publicist asked as I stood in the chill and din of Lumaville. Since she worked in-house, she had nothing to prove, whereas the pay-to-play firms are always cooking up results to justify their retainer.

I told her where I worked. She didn't recognize the masthead so I elaborated that it was a network of local-centric news sites. We both sighed.

I heard the clickety clack of a keyboard in the background. I was being vetted.

"And you're on the transportation beat?" she asked. "You're in the system as art and lifestyle. And 'other.'"

"That's the one," I said. "Transportation is part of my other."

"Make a girl feel real special there, Howell."

The *system* was one of two PR contact management services on the market. They're vast databases that aggregate the names, affiliations and contact information of every journo under the sun and sell online access on a subscription basis. Since the proliferation of bloggers, social media marketing and other related hoo-haw, such services have merged with press release services that promise backlinks and guaranteed access to "influentials." On our side of the gig, what it amounts to is a whole lot of spam and hours lost in the newsroom deleting releases for drink recipes and "survivor" books by "experts" of every stripe.

"And it was murals you wanted to talk about?" she asked.

"Murals and security. How does your surveillance system keep the artwork from being vandalized?" I asked. I was dog-paddling but I was doing it well.

"Oh, I can answer that," she said, her tone brightening. I didn't need a spokesperson. I wanted to get in the security room and slip an underpaid, overworked, bleary–eyed security tech twenty bucks to run some video for me. But that wasn't her problem. Her job consisted of telling chumps like me that the cars had new seats or that they express their condolences to the family of the guy who jumped in front of the train at the depot. Otherwise, it's damage control, like when a SMART cop shoots a minority, or a kid, or both.

"First off, as you probably know, we have cameras that help provide a safe and comfortable travel environment for our clients..."

She had downshifted into PR speak. Autopilot.

"Those same cameras, of course, surveil the installations to ensure that the overall consumer experience is one of pleasure and convenience. We, of course, also want to extend the greatest effort to our community artists to ensure that their contribution to the SMART experience is accorded the respect that it deserves," she continued.

"So, in some ways the guys watching the security cameras are like docents in a museum?" I asked.

"Yes, yes, I like that. Docents."

"Keep it, on the house," I said, then added with a bit of cheek, "Can I speak to one of the docents?"

There was a bit of a pause. Then bingo:

"You know, I have just the guy for you – he's a painter or something at the U but does part-time hours with us in security," she said. "He'd be perfect. Multi-culti and a cutie too. There are going to be images, right?"

"Absolutely. I'll take them myself."

"You're not sending a photographer?" she asked, incredulous, then answered her own question. "Oh, right, it's a blog. Duh. I always forget you guys do everything on an iPhone."

It was true. I did nearly everything on an iPhone. I'd even taken to occasionally using a foldable keyboard to give my thumbs a rest. Then I'd go back to the laptop to give my eyes a rest. Then I'd go to the bar and give my brain a rest. But not anymore.

I told the PR woman I was on a tight deadline and asked if I could meet the student artist security dude today. She was asked for my mobile number and said she'd text me shortly.

I was getting good at this low-grade detective bullshit. If I hadn't gone for the lifestyle beat, I might've been an investigative journalist – but then, naturally, I would have to have been a journalist first and frankly I never was. I've never been a reporter, just a writer in a reporter's jacket. But had I the heavens' embroidered cloths...

22.
Smoke

Adriane's text was to the point:

'Where the duck is my story?"

Autocorrect was turning her fucks into ducks. After two more attempts she gave up, which is just as well since I didn't have her ducking story yet.

"You're popular," Annika said of the series of dings as we pulled in front of my apartment, which used to be ours.

"It's my editor. I got her to stick her neck out for me. While her head was in a bucket."

"That tracks, anatomically, I guess." Annika gave the ebrake a yank. I never used it but realized in that moment that the women I knew always did. I looked at the last text and decided to turn off my phone instead. We watched the phone go through its routine for a silent eternity.

"So, you coming up?" I finally said.

Annika pretended that she wasn't expecting it. She wrinkled her nose as if in pain. "Um, why?" she said.

"To get your piano." Good save, Daedalus Howell.

She closed her eyes and nodded. Then she let some air escape through teeth, which I decided was something like a laugh. Humor was always my secret weapon with her.

Annika straightened her back to take a deep view in the

rearview mirror.

"Okay, I'll get my piano," she said. "This time."

"And you should know, the place is a wreck."

"I'll close my eyes while you make the bed."

* * *

Upstairs, Annika and I waded through the dross of my upturned life. Mostly paper as it turns out. I had a habit of printing drafts of everything I ever wrote just in case the Internet went out. Now I saw what a shitty idea that was – posterity scattered all over the floor like a game of 52-Card Pickup.

"This place is one matchstick from being a bonfire, Fergus."

"I'm glad you see it has potential," I said as I pulled the cork from a bottle of Audacious Red.

I poured two glasses. Rather, I poured one wine glass for Annika and a sort of tumbler for me, which sometimes doubled as an ashtray. We drank. It was a cheap, quaffable plonk I knew from my days as a wine columnist, before winos got hip to blogging and put us all out of business.

"Probably shouldn't smoke in here," Annika said as she tamped a cigarette on her wrist. Given the fire hazard and the fact I was drinking out of the ashtray, I agreed. "Come to the window with me."

This was Annika's old trick – she'd throw up the sash, plant her ass on the sill and dangle her legs over the edge. She poked her head out the window but decided to hover there a moment rather than dangle.

"When are you going to the SMART Train?" she said out of the side of her mouth as she lit up.

"Scheduled an interview early tomorrow," I said. "I'll

need some cash since I plan to bribe the guy to show me the time–coded video."

"No problem. Should I go with?"

Part of me thought I shouldn't let her out of my sight but another part was getting tired of looking at her. That's the problem with being pretty, it's like a light bulb you can't turn off. Her chunky black glasses only served to frame her looks and on cue she took them off as my eyes lingered on hers.

Either the mask was off or the blindfold was on — Annika was nearsighted and blind without her specs. I assumed there was something she didn't want to see and the wine got me thinking it was herself revealed in my eyes. She was no longer the woman I loved but someone who had stepped into darkness the same way I had stumbled a shade into the light. Now that we were further apart we could finally see each other. But not for who we were, but for what we never thought we could become.

She walked backward, her palms stretched behind her until they connected with the keys of the piano and made a monstrous chord. Smoke from her cigarette rose from behind her and limned her silhouette.

"I have coffee, wine and cigarette breath," she said. That meant I had coffee, wine and cigarette breath too. "Proceed at your own risk."

I reached around her slender waist to the ancient tin of mints where the piano's music rack once was. Inside was a cone of incense, a guitar pick, a wine charm I mistook for an earring and two fossilized tablets that could either be mints or aspirin. I offered her the tin and Annika nearly ate the wine charm. I gave her one of the fossil mints instead and took one for myself. It tasted like nag champa incense, which is to say it tasted like a college dorm in the nineties.

We ground the mints like a pair of cement mixers. Mine

turned out to be aspirin and required a swig of wine to choke down, mooting the whole damn exercise.

"This doesn't change anything," she whispered.

"If I wanted change I'd go to a laundromat."

"You should go anyway," she said as she put a hand on my chest and smeared my buttons around a while. "What's this?"

She used her index finger and weird thumb to gap my button–up so she could see what was beneath – a superman shirt.

"I gave you this, didn't I? It's ancient."

"So are we."

"Speak for yourself. 40 is the new black," she said.

The first kiss was glancing. The second more purposeful. The third was an attempt to recall what it used to be and the fourth went wee wee wee all the way home.

I didn't bother making the bed. Or making love, per se.

Even after all the years, on and off, Annika Strang remained some kind of archetype, all anima and Jungian wet dreams. And this was precisely why she shouldn't be with me.

I was a tourist, not a fellow traveler. After our last break up I apologized for never getting to know her and she apologized for never being herself. Now there was no other Troy for her to burn, just smoky breath and the charnel house of memory. We didn't make love, we made peace, which is really just making do when it's already done.

23.
To Catch a Train

I sputtered into the phone.

"Daedalus Howell."

I announced myself when I answered so whoever called knew how to pronounce my name. Which they summarily forgot. Only bill collectors with liberal arts educations remembered.

"Got you the muralist," said the SMART Train's PR woman.

I rolled over. Annika was gone. And – some–fucking–how – so was her piano.

"You can meet with Ray Murgia anytime that's convenient to you," she said and gave me his number, which I scratched into a bedside reporter's notebook with a fading Pilot G–2 07 clickable pen. Its line was – as my college roommate said of his preferred type of coed – not too fat, not too fine. I wondered what happened to that roommate, then I remembered; what a hot mess that was.

"He's there now," said the publicist. "I'd love to get a link to the clip when it's live."

Link to the clip? Even PR lingo was defying physics these days.

"What's your deadline, by the way?"

Deadline? Ah, yes – I was on deadline. A quantum deadline. Get it together, man. "Today," I said. One of us hung up.

I waded through the ankle-deep wood pulp that amounted to my life's work and set my eyes on the spot where Annika's piano once was. In its place was a to-go cup of coffee and a vegan chocolate donut sprinkled with shaved coconut. I grabbed the coffee – too hot, then the donut – just right – and read the inscription on the napkin: "Downstairs. Got kid's phone. Works! – A." She finished the note with a flourish of musical notes.

I buttoned a whitish shirt over my bluish T–shirt, pulled on yesterday's jeans and my new blazer. I felt exactly how I did on the occasions that I woke up in the Mini – disheveled, relieved and elsewhere. I had no idea how far I'd take that concept in the next 12 hours.

* * *

As promised, Annika was seated outside at the cafe. We once wasted an entire afternoon arguing over whether the table was British Racing Green or some other verdant hue. Her pale skin reflected whatever it was, casting her in an eerie iridescent glow. She almost looked healthy, like Osiris after a good sleep.

"Well?" said Annika as I folded into the seat across from hers. "Aren't you gonna ask?"

"Where's Jude?"

"Jude is fine," she said crisply. "I know he's fine. You have to believe me. And it gets better." She brightened some. "The piano."

Right.

"Where's the piano?"

"I don't know," she said with a sardonic smile.

"I can live with that," I said and I sipped the coffee that had finally cooled.

Annika folded her arms and stared at me.

"I hacked the phone – Ashe's phone. I hacked the Easter Egg in 'The Knights of Skeldaria' just like our boy. And you know what? It worked. I was smart enough to offset the phone's geolocation by a couple of feet; otherwise, you know, it would've been me and not the piano sent into some parallel universe."

This — this is why I will never sleep next to Annika Strang again. I don't have enough square footage to feel safe from being hurled into realms unknown.

"Wait, so you sent a half ton of Sitka spruce and elephant parts into some other universe and you –"

"THOSE weren't ivory keys," she yelled, recoiling. "I'd never have a piano with ivory keys. Who do you think I am? They were probably cellulose or something."

"Did you maybe consider who your piano might've landed on?"

"It didn't land on anybody."

"What if it landed on an elephant? Would that at least give you pause?"

"It doesn't work like that," she said. "It simply went from your apartment to another version of your apartment in another universe."

She wasn't convincing to either of us. I shook my head.

"What would Einstein do?" I asked.

"Math."

"Sure and what about 'God doesn't play dice with the universe' and shit? Just because God's not playing doesn't mean it ain't a crapshoot, thanks to people like you and Cameron and everyone else rolling Snake Eyes with your gadgets and hubris…"

Annika laughed that ugly, brilliant laugh of hers. She wasn't used to me having the moral upper–hand.

"Gadgets and Hubris?" she appraised, raising an eyebrow. She pulled a smoke from her pack with her teeth, lit it. "Sounds like a band from the 90s, Day-Dal-Us. Burn me a disc and we'll drop Ecstasy and talk all night about being latchkey kids."

I put the key to the Mini on the cafe table. And drank my coffee. Annika looped the keyring around her weird thumb.

"I take it I'm driving."

"Yep," I said between sips.

"Downtown?"

"SMART Train headquarters," I said. "I need to think."

"Don't hurt yourself."

We sat for a moment, quiet. I tried not to hurt myself but every thought I had came back like a bludgeon of self–doubt.

"Incidentally, there's only a one in thirty-six chance to roll Snake Eyes," she said.

Somehow, that wasn't reassuring.

* * *

SMART headquarters was formed by two gigantic slabs of concrete that decided to mate but passed out halfway through. The rest was tiled, even the front desk behind which was a large woman who filled the semicircular space as if she had waded into a jacuzzi that was a few sizes too small. Her arms rested atop the perimeter of her station, palms down. She looked like a made man wedged into his corner booth mugging for the camera – which would've been more pleasant, I thought, as I presented my credentials and namedropped Ray Murgia the security guard and moonlighting muralist.

She nodded, then tossed her chins toward Annika, who flinched.

"Who's she?"

"My photographer," I said instinctively.

"No pictures of the security room," she said to me. Annika didn't interest her. She pushed a clipboard toward me. Her long fingernails were well–manicured and chartreuse.

I signed my name to the ledger and passed it to Annika.

"She doesn't need to sign. Just put a 'plus one' next to your name."

I used to "plus one" Annika back in the days I got comp'd to live music shows. It was a cheap date burnished with a sense of privilege. That all dried up when the music industry tanked and YouTube links became the common currency, which just isn't as sexy.

I put a plus-one next to my name. The woman told us to take the elevator to the third floor and take a right. I thanked her and she glowered back as she wriggled goodbye with her fingers. Her nails clicked like cricket's legs.

Upstairs, the door to the security office was heavy and smudged. A sign kindly suggested that we dispose of food and beverages. I ignored it and continued clutching my coffee. The door opened before I could knock.

"What, are you psychic?" I asked.

Ray Murguia was a twenty-something beardling with broad smile and his hair carefully clipped into a flat top.

"Don't need to be psychic," he said with a laugh. "I've got more cameras here than a fly has eyes."

"Like Argus," Annika said.

Ugh. Shut up, Annika, I thought.

"Who's Argus?"

"Greek myth. Guard with a thousand eyes," she said.

"Gotcha," Ray said as he dropped back into his seat in the small, airless office. The room was lit by a bank of flat screen monitors bolted to the wall. The light fluttered in a shade of blue and reflected off his stainless steel desk. He reeked of weed and the body spray he hoped would cover it. "That'd be a sweet tag," he said. He repeated "Argus" several times under his breath, trying it on.

"So, you're what the SMART train brass call a 'community artist,'" I said.

Ray rolled his eyes.

"It sounds better than 'graffiti artist,' right?"

I smiled and launched my phone's recording app and angled the phone on the desk. Ray froze.

"Ah, shit. You're gonna record this?" he said.

I nodded.

"I don't know why you wanna talk to me for the news, man. I haven't even had a show yet. In fact, I'm kind of not ready to reveal my next big thing until it's actually the next big thing. You know what I mean? I mean, I don't wanna be ungrateful..." he said and continued to ramble but less coherently.

He was stoned.

I waved my hand slowly in the air to wind him down and slipped my phone back in my pocket.

"Okay, Ray, we can raincheck 'til you're ready. But I'll need a favor then," I said.

Annika rolled up her sleeves and slipped behind Ray's chair. She knelt down, her eyes on the screen.

"Brilliant, bro. Cool," Ray said. "I'm doing these really, really big installations and they're just not done and –"

I waved my hand again. He calmed down.

"I need to see some video – security video."

"For the article?" he said, then added as if apologizing, "You know I can't do that, bro."

I put my coffee cup on Ray's desk, reached into my pocket and flipped open my reporter's notebook. I jotted the time and date, tore out the page and wafted it onto his desk.

"I think you can," I said.

Ray squinted back at me. He wasn't used to being squeezed. Not that it bothered him, it just wasn't something he knew how to answer. Annika had a better idea. She sprung up with a baggie plucked from the pocket of the coat slung on Ray's chair. She dipped in with her thumb – that thumb – and forefinger, and plucked a joint from the foliage.

I was impressed with her stealth. Ray less so. His big, dumb smile contorted into a grimace of fear and loathing.

"Shit. So, this is how it is. You're cool, right?" he asked, a quaver in his voice.

"What do you think?" Annika asked as she lit the joint. She had a tug and exhaled in his face.

Ray sighed as if he too was exhaling, which he was a moment later after Annika passed him the joint. Accord was found.

"Alright then. What route are we talking about?"

"Lumaville," I told him.

Ray checked the time and date on the notebook and clicked through a few folders on his computer. He opened a few files and after a moment a video popped up on screen. It was clear vantage of the interior of a train car, then another and another, all hitched together like pictures in a zoetrope.

"You know what you're looking for?"

"Yeah."

"'Know it when you see it' sort of thing?"

"A boy, about twelve wearing a navy blue school blazer. He's in trouble."

"Shit, man, I used to get in trouble on the train too. Never gave them my real name," Ray smiled. Then he turned to Annika. "What was that eyeball guy again?"

"Argus," Annika said.

"Argus," Ray repeated. "Good tag. Gonna use that."

Annika was chuffed. Her wicked smile revealed only her canines. She relished small victories, like a priest making his quota on deathbed conversions.

Unlike the surveillance footage of yore, the video was clean, full color and in high definition images, slightly fisheyed from the wide angle lens.

Ray slowly rolled the trackball mouse at his right and scrubbed through the video. No Jude. He pulled up another video, again nothing. After a few more I got the idea I was on the wrong path. Then...

"Holy shit," Ray said under his breath.

"What is it?"

"Look at this," he said.

We all leaned into the monitor. He dragged his cursor over the image, which made it larger. He cued up the slider and hit the spacebar on his computer. The video played in double time. People got off and on the train at the herky–jerky pace of an undercranked silent film: business men and women, elderly people, teenagers, bicyclists and then – out of nowhere – Jude, in his blue blazer, streaked across the screen.

"Did you see that?" Ray asked.

"That's him," I said.

"But did you see this..." Ray rewound the video and slowed it down.

The scene played out again except this time we could see plainly that Jude didn't run into the frame from offscreen – he just appeared in the middle of the image, suddenly, and out of nowhere.

"Was there a break in the video feed or something?"

Annika asked.

"No, that's the thing – look at the time code."

"You're sure?"

Ray played the sequence again, even slower. Again, Jude appeared out of nowhere, like a jump-cut, like an edit in a Buntel Eriksson flick. But the numbers that scrolled at the bottom of the screen never broke sequence. There were no breaks, just time moving fluidly forward.

"That's impossible," Ray said.

"Give me your pen," said Annika. I handed it to her and she reached for the notebook page on Ray's desk.

She was off by a centimeter. My coffee cup tipped over, lost its lid, and a brew-nami flooded the keyboard.

"Fuck!" Annika spat as she tried to contain the mess with her sleeve.

Ray reeled back in his seat as coffee rained a black waterfall over the edge of his desk. A puddle grew on the floor as Ray paced the tiny office.

The screen was black. The image of Jude and the timecode was gone.

"Now what?" I said, which didn't help but felt like a contribution nonetheless.

Annika balled her fist. I wasn't sure who she was going to hit – me or Ray, who was rapidly running his hands through his hair on the verge of panic.

She hit the screen. The image came back – Jude running, timecode and all. Annika scribbled the eight-part number, broken into double-digit pairs by colons. Day, hour, minute, second. She had what she needed to get Jude back.

"Got it," she said.

"Got what?" Ray had lost his shit. "I mean, really, who the fuck are you people?"

I put my hand on his shoulder and looked him in the eye.

"It's cool, man. We're the news."

24.
Well Hung

Annika made me drive, which was annoying because she was the one who always knew where to go. Not this time. She rode shotgun and every few minutes tapped "call" on her phone's screen, and let it ring out, until she was greeted by the same outgoing message: "This is Cameron Block. Don't bother leaving a message. If I wanted to talk to you, I would have answered. Have a nice day."

Annika sighed and put her phone to sleep.

I turned another corner to nowhere.

"Why won't he answer?" she said, simmering.

"According to his message, he doesn't want to talk to you."

She shot me a withering glance.

"He's making me jump through hoops," she said. "To make sure he can still trust me."

"Why wouldn't he trust you?"

Annika stared at me blankly: "Well, last night for starters."

Of course, that, whatever that was.

I almost said "What he doesn't know won't hurt him," which is what a man in my dubious position is supposed to say but I didn't feel dubious enough to bother. But then I thought – what if he does know? What if I'm being played by Cameron through Annika. She was a tricksy hobbit but not that tricksy. And in point of fact, he couldn't trust her. Least of all with sex. But if he couldn't trust her, why should I?

Because, as Jude's only hope, she was my only hope.

"I really fucked this up," she said. Her voice broke midway and she teared up. The more she resisted, the more her eyes welled up, until, when she finally blinked, tears cascaded over her long lashes as if from the downspout of a rain gutter.

I didn't like it when she cried because I never knew what motivated it. I used to do the usual twenty questions until I once conjectured about her menstrual cycle and she ashed her cigarette in my coffee. I offered to call Cameron myself.

"You think he would answer a call from you and not me?" she said, incredulous. "There are so many pieces to this puzzle, Daedalus Howell. You and I are just pieces."

That no longer fit together.

I pulled over and hovered the Mini by a fire hydrant. I took out the phone. On the screen was an email notification. I opened it and was greeted by a familiar tone. At this point, I almost welcomed it:

"*Dead-alas Howl. I'm your biggest fan. A-part-from-you,*" it read – creepy hyphens and all. "*Culture vulture, journalistic gigolo, pay-to-play rewriter of press releases, come to this hallowed place where my friends' portraits hang and look thereon…*"

A jpeg was attached to the email, an image from a gallery, a scanned postcard. It was titled "An Hero." The bad grammar was intentional – it was, as the Editrix once schooled me, Internet slang for "suicide." I have no idea why, but I no longer doubted her veracity since the tag below the title read "Suicide Portraiture." This was inscribed over an acrylic fiasco of some sadsack whose tongue was covered with little white pills arranged like billiard balls. It was an advertisement for a show of student works at some shithole downtown and if I knew anything about pharmaceuticals, I knew that a couple dozen five-mil pills of Lorazepam wouldn't meet the so-called "minimum lethal dose." So much for truth in advertising. But what do I know? I'm not a doctor, nor do I play one on TV, which makes me doubly ignorant.

I sighed and Annika asked why, so I showed her.

She raised an eyebrow.

"The date," she said.

"Yeah, I guess we missed the opening. Too bad – could've gotten five hundred words out of it and a some free wine," I muttered. "Used to be my beat."

"No, the 'timestamp' on the email."

"Yesterday, right? I haven't been up on my email. I've got a whole folder devoted to my 'biggest fan' brimming with hate mail – you know, in case I'm found face-down in the river wearing a debutante dress."

"No one would suspect foul play," she said, then got serious. "The date is from five years ago."

"What?" I said. "I know you think I'm a loser but it's definitely been less than five years since I checked my email."

Annika tapped the date on the phone with her weird thumb.

"You know what day that is, right?"

I puzzled on it a moment. But it didn't take long. It was the end date chiseled into 1K's useless gravestone.

"What the hell?"

Annika wiped her eyes with the heels of her palms.

She didn't need to tell me where to go. I pulled the Mini back into traffic and gunned it up the boulevard.

* * *

The gallery was on Washington and near Telephone Alley. It was a tidy space with the requisite white walls and cement floor and was a bright spot on the block that I decided was a cultural black hole. I never went to this part of Lumaville because A) once the Thai joint ignored my request to forgo the fish sauce and I went into anaphylactic shock; and B) I wasn't needful of a women's gym and if I was I wouldn't go to one that required I workout in the storefront window in front of ogling men; C) the Thai joint didn't believe me when I faked going into anaphylactic shock when I was really just squeamish about fish and D) I was browbeat for ogling women in the storefront window when, in fact, I was checking out my own reflection.

I parked in front. Annika assisted by pulling the emergency brake, then put her hands in her lap and sat motionless looking out the window into the gutter. To anyone else she might have looked half catatonic but I knew she was thinking, wandering the dark corridors of that great mind of hers looking for bread crumbs. I figured I was going in solo and I undid my seatbelt but left the key in the ignition in case Annika wanted to turn on the air conditioner or the airwaves. I opened the car door.

"Wait," she said. Her hand was on my wrist. "Leave me the phone."

I began to rethink leaving the keys in the ignition.

"Why?"

"I have an idea. I need that email," she said. Her affect was flat, like her voice. All of her mental resources were working on a bigger challenge than intonation or being good company. "You have to trust me."

I didn't want to but I had to and she knew it and knew it bothered me. She tried again.

"He means as much to me as he does to you," she said, her personality coming back like blood to a sleeping limb.

"Who?" I said, "Cameron or Jude?"

* * *

Inside the gallery, the walls were bare, though occasional nails poked out like whiskers missed in a shave. I presumed paintings were once there. A young woman in her early twenties was tidying up with a push broom and an unlit hand-rolled cigarette stuck to a moist spot on her lip.

A blow-up of the "An Hero" advert was pegged to an easel. When the women noticed us, she plucked the earbuds from her head and crossed to us. She was small and scrubby with an A-line bob and a kaleidoscope of paint caked on her hands that looked like she had just given Jackson Pollack a hand job. She wore arty, unattractive glasses, by design I assumed, and she smiled a lot. Way too much for a person of her generation, if my Editrix and the miserable Edwyn were representative of the species.

"Show over?" I said, looking around the gallery.

"Is now," she said and patted the pocket of her smock. A handwritten check with at least four zeroes poked over the top of her pocket.

"I sold them all, if that's why you're here," she said as she gestured to the walls. She wasn't smug, or proud or particularly interested into what amounted to a windfall for any artist, let alone a recent Art Department refugee.

"I'm not here to buy a painting," I said, while reaching into my coat pocket.

"Then, what, are you a cop?" She plucked the cigarette from

her lip and wiped away the bangs pasted to her brow. Below was a constellation of freckles.

"No, I'm a reporter. Well, a blogger, or whatever" I said, flashing my reporter's notebook. "I heard about the sale. Congrats. Can I get a quote?"

She smiled, put the cigarette back and foraged her smock for a light, "Sure thing. But do I have to talk about painting?"

"You're a painter, aren't you?" I asked. What's with these freaking kids' reluctance to chat up the press? One would sooner get a kidney than a quote. Which could be useful, I thought.

"I'm not a painter anymore," she said. She sat on a folding chair and gestured for me to do the same.

"Quitting while you're ahead?" I joked.

She thought I was referring to the cigarette.

"More like now I can do what I really want to do, which is make apps."

My expression was blank a second too long. She sidled up beside me and whipped her phone from her smock pocket. Smocket? Nevermind.

She swiped the screen and a cartoon chicken appeared of the sort that might appear as marginalia in a cookbook.

"Nice. It's a chicken, right?" I said.

She poked it with a paint-stained finger. The chicken exploded. In it's place was a pile of writhing, animated worms.

"It was a chicken," she said. "Now, it's a plague."

She leaned back in her chair, finally proud.

"This is what I really want to do."

"Blow up chickens?"

"And get the fuck out of art school," she said. "It's all about games now."

"Who bought all the paintings?" I asked.

"I don't know. Collectors. Suckers," she said. "I'm not sure why anyone would buy them. I'm not much of a painter," she admitted. She pointed to the poster on the easel and could tell I agreed. She smiled an impish smile.

"Suicide portraiture. Your idea?" I said. "Kind of macabre, don't you think?"

"It was a required assignment for a required show with a required gallery show. We got pictures of dead people off news sites and painted them. Gross, right?"

I shrugged.

"Preston took the ones with guns. I did jumpers."

"Jumpers?"

"Bridge jumpers. And pills. I did pills, too," she said. "Preston was supposed to be the star. And he should be. I'm afraid I sort of upset the cosmic balance of the painting department. This is off the record, right?"

"Yeah, no worries. I just want to know who bought them. Are you sure it wasn't a single collector?"

She gave me the once over, then reiterated, "This is still off the record?"

"I'll let you know when it's on the record."

"Okay, only because I don't want people thinking I was fucking him or anything. Because I didn't. But one guy, an old guy, I mean old like you, not totally decrepit, but older, came in and bought everything on the walls. He would've bought the fire extinguisher if I had thought to put my name on it," she said. "My name is Edie. It's on the wall."

It was.

"You didn't know him?"

"No. All I know is that Preston, the golden boy, basically had his ass handed to him by the karma police," said Edie.

"Who's Preston?" I asked, flipping open my notebook. "This is still off the record, by the way."

"Good, because it sucks. For Preston. He was my show mate. He's the guy at school that everyone thought was the shit – almost as much as he thought he was the shit. It was his big night. I was just soy filler, if you know what I mean," she explained. "Then, little red 'sold' signs started going up on my work. At that point, the energy in the party totally changed. Preston sold, like, one painting to his step–dad or something. I sold everything. In fifteen minutes. Preston was so humiliated he chucked all his gun paintings in the dumpster. Somebody should fish them out because they'll be worth something. Someday."

"That's my next stop," I said. "But all your paintings went to the same collector?"

Edie nodded.

"I took a picture of the check and texted it to my mom," she said. Then she pulled the original from her top pocket and held it to my nose.

It was from FMRL and it was signed "C. Block."

Sonofabitch.

"You know who that is, right?"

"Sounds like a wing in a prison to me," she said. "Or maybe it stands for 'Cock Block.'"

I was beginning to like her.

"Cameron Block," I said.

She rolled her eyes.

"You mean the dude who did 'The Knights of Skeldaria?' Oh, fuck. Really?" she said. She slapped the constellation on her forehead.

"Cameron take the art with him?"

Edie slouched in her chair, dumbfounded by her brush with tech–celebrity.

"No, man, he had me crate and deliver it to a storage unit across town," she said. "Paid extra, too."

She sighed and looked blue, splayed in her chair like a rag doll.

"What?" I asked. "Wish you priced your paintings higher?"

"That's not it," she said. "I don't really care about the money.

I wish I'd asked him for a job – I would do it for free."

I got off the folding chair. It stuck to my ass for second before peeling back to the floor.

"You still can ask him for a job," I said, and added, "By the way, a job you do for free is called an internship. Don't be an intern."

"Okay," she said, sitting up.

"You want his number?"

"Yes," she said. She leaned forward.

"Where's the storage unit?"

"You mean his storage unit? I don't think I'm supposed to tell you that."

"Fair enough," I said and made for the door. But not convincingly. I had to revert to "slow motion" as Edie just stared at me going through the motion of walking out, very slowly.

"Okay, okay, your hardball pantomime convinced me," she said.

Edie snatched my reporter's notebook from my hand and waited for me to hand her a pen. I did and she scrawled an address. I reciprocated by writing Cameron's email from memory onto the lower half of the page then ripped it out for her.

"Good luck playing chicken," I said as I made for the door for real.

"You too," she said.

Back on the sidewalk, diners frowned and shrugged at a menu taped in the Thai joint's window. Next door, women stared far off into their futures as they strode treadmills en route to wherever it was those women were headed. I took the key for the Mini from my coat pocket and stood on the curb, dick in my hand – the Mini was gone. And Annika with it.

25.
Storage

Annika and the Mini were across the street, which was where the streetcleaner wasn't. I watched the behemoth sputter down the avenue as it gave the gutter a wash and brush up and was pleased to know Lumaville kept its curbsides clean, especially with the cost of dry cleaning and my propensity to lie down on the job.

I gestured to Annika to do another U-ey, which would technically be an O-ey, all things considered. She ignored me and continued hacking the phone, deep into the mysteries of my email. It made me regret figuring out how to route my email to it in the first place. For a moment I worried she would find the breadcrumbs of some recent Craigslist flameouts in the Casual Encounters department but then I remembered I used a bogus name, fake email address and a mugshot photoshopped on my erstwhile laptop. Basically, I played Cyrano to a fictional character who mysteriously never got laid. Then there was all my pathetic exchanges with Crysta the Barista, which I saved in a folder called "Start Here" on the off-chance she murdered me and the cops needed a leg up.

If Annika was onto my online shenanigans she didn't let on. Instead, a small smile curved around her canines and she whipped the car around in a single, fluid arc. I got in.

"I know where they are," Annika said as she pulled back into the afternoon traffic. "And I think I know how to get there."

I slapped the piece of paper that Edie, the artist-turned-Exploder-of-Fowl, gave me onto the dash as if I was raising the ante.

"I've got a lead too," I said. "And I know how to get there."

Annika shook her head even before her eyes had darted over the address.

"That's not it," she said. "Cameron and Jude aren't there. Not even remotely. Not even the right dimension."

I pegged the paper down with my finger as Annika made a sharp turn.

"If this address isn't even in the right dimension we can assume it's closer then," I said, putting my crappy card on the table, even though Annika and I weren't playing the same game. She had a royal flush and I had to "go fish."

Since Annika was driving, I had to make my case.

"Cam just bought a shit-ton of art and he's hoarding it at this location. Who knows what else he's got there. Or who else," I said.

Annika tapped on the interior clock of the Mini.

"Let me explain this in terms you'll understand," she said. She spoke slowly to make it stick: "We're on 'deadline.' If we don't make our deadline, then everything we've been trying to accomplish will be over. And Jude will be over. And I'll be over. And you, well, you're some kind of karmic cockroach so who knows what will happen to you. But it'll be bad and you will regret it." She was no longer talking to me so much as her own icy eyes in the rearview mirror.

"Fifteen minutes, just fifteen" I said, then added the jab, "What's fifteen minutes in the face of infinity minus one?"

"Sometimes fifteen minutes can seem infinite," she said as she eased the pedal to the floor. I tried to decode her subtext but couldn't decide whether she was referring to the fifteen minutes of fame I achieved after 1K jumped off the bridge or our sexploits from the night before.

"You know where you're going?" I asked.

"I read the address," she said. "What is it?"

"It's a storage unit.

Annika's look of disdain lingered long enough for her to have to swerve when her eyes were back on the road.

"I'm a reporter for crissakes. Trust my instincts," I said. "There's something in that storage unit and it isn't just portraits of suicides."

"Every second we waste there puts us that much closer to failing. You know what that means don't you?" she said. "That boy has to get back before the quantum deadline. An infinite amount of causalities, timelines and even entire realities are at stake."

Annika's alabaster cheeks blotched the salmon hue that meant she was angry. She pulled off the road and into a parking lot with little heed for the speed bumps that thudded beneath us.

The building was broad and beige and ugly in a predictably inoffensive way. Any PC on a desk from the 1990s could serve as a scale model. Inside, the place buzzed with overly bright fluorescence. Presiding over the counter was a walking dermatology appointment whose faded black concert shirt peeked from under the edges of a short-sleeve denim work shirt. The storage chain's logo, some sort of impossible cube nicked from Escher, was embroidered on his pocket. Apparently, Cam was as susceptible to brand identification as anyone and a simple box wouldn't do.

The undercover rocker at the counter barely acknowledged we were in the room, let alone question whether or not we had the customer keycode that summoned the elevator. Which we didn't. Annika approached the pad by the elevator buttons and entered a flurry of digits. After a few false tries, some combo worked and the elevator doors opened. I waited until we were in and the doors were closed again before I indicated how impressed I was.

"It was a hunch. Cam used the same password at the office. For everything," she said. "RVW2."

"What's RVW2?" I asked.

"I have no idea," she said.

"It sounds like the 'morning after' pill."

"No, it doesn't," Annika said archly.

"Or a tax form," I added. "Or a World War II era Winnebago."

"No such thing," she said. "And it's offensive to the Ho-Chunk Nation of Wisconsin to say 'Winnebago.'"

"Why?"

"It's an 'exonym' – a name made up for an ethnic group by outsiders."

"Okay, no 'W' word," I said, then muttered "Wikipedia" under my breath.

"I heard that," Annika grumbled.

The elevator doors opened onto a maze of nondescript hallways. Annika squinted a moment then led me by the arm to the right, then left, then right, then left, then left, then I couldn't keep track anymore. The halls were lined with orange roll-up doors and behind each, I presumed, was a heap of crap, the banker-boxed dross of consumerism, a gross spectrum of stowage, from the practical to the sentimental, and shades of hoarding in between. What might comprise the overstock of Cameron Block's perfect life?

The entire combustible world in one small room.

Annika crouched down in front of one of the orange

doors and started working on the combination lock.

"You know the combo?"

"Eighteen twenty-two, twenty-three," she said. "Same letters by their number in the alphabet."

"What are you doing in Lumaville? You should be at Bletchley Park cracking Enigma," I said. She was not amused. She stepped back and invited me to pull a muscle by rolling the door up from the floor.

"Why me?"

"In case it's booby trapped," she said, then added with a smirk, "I'm too valuable to the war effort."

After the first yank, the orange door levitated from my fingers and rolled tidily up a pair of tracks.

The joint was packed, neatly, with plastic cubes the size of dorm room refrigerators that interlocked like ginormous Legos. Leave it to Cameron to acquire some next-generation Scandinavian personal organization system. They were probably sourced from reclaimed materials too – like the broken dreams of cardboard box manufacturers or the market anxieties of those who design closet shoe racks.

The boxes were arranged such that there was a pathway that formed a kind of spiral, like a snail shell.

"Holy shit," said Annika.

"Yeah, the guy's pretty anal," I said. I directed her eyes to the barcode stickers on each plastic box.

"And organized," she deadpanned. She frowned. "You don't see it, do you?"

"The organization? I'm a chaos-man myself, so this is just vanilla to me," I said.

"He's set it up like a Golden Spiral, based on the Golden Ratio..." she was going to keep digging until I got it, which meant we'd arrive in China someday. I caught a break when she asked, "What's in these?"

That was my cue to open a box. I chose some low-hanging fruit near the back. I snapped the lid off a box that was thigh-high. It was dark in the unit, but after a moment my eyes adjusted and the contents of the box revealed themselves. Wine. Several cases of Audacious Red. It was cheap but "quaffable," as we say in the trade (I was once a wine critic for about fifteen minutes) but not the kind of plonk anyone would cellar. Why was Cam building up such a stash? What did he know that we didn't? Did he expect a dearth of red table wine after the zombie apocalypse?

Annika began to forage on her own as I slipped a bottle of Audacious Red into my coat pocket. Its neck stuck out to my elbow, but as long as I tucked my hand under my lapel like Napoleon it wouldn't be a bother.

"Look familiar?" Annika asked as she exhumed a canvas from another plastic box. The reek of linseed oil was strong. The painting was fresh – not even dry. And of course, it looked familiar. It was a portrait of 1K as interpreted by Edie, a.k.a Poultrygeist.

"I don't know what's creepier – the fact that she painted it, or the fact that Cameron Block owns it."

"Who knows what motivates artists. But I know what motivates Cam," she said. "All this – these are futures."

She could see I was confused.

"In the financial sense. These are investments. They're time capsules."

"Even the wine?" I said as I slipped a bottle in my other pocket. Symmetry seemed to demand it.

"He's probably aging it by using the app like a time machine."

I rolled my eyes.

"Time machines. They get old fast," I said. "And the art?"

"Same thing."

"Somewhere, sometime this chick is probably Van Gogh."

"How do you know?"

"I don't. But Cam probably does," she said. "And I bet he's been there."

I tried to pry open another box, but the lid was connected to other lids, and then I realized it was actually a big box camouflaged as many smaller ones. Altogether, the lid was the size of a door on its side. With some oomph, the lid came off and fell to the floor. Inside the big box was not the couple cases of Audacious Red I expected. It was a coffin – or something like a coffin. It was more of a metal sarcophagus draped in an ivy of tubes and wire. It could pass for an iron lung. But whoever, or whatever, inside of it wasn't breathing. There was a porthole on top that looked like it was salvaged from the Yellow Submarine and through its thick pane was a face – or at least what used to be a face. The visage was strewn with frost and had a metallic sheen. Its owner had wandered so deep into the uncanny valley I was hard-pressed to call it human.

I didn't scream, in part, because I didn't know what the hell I was looking at. Annika did and let out a B-film-worthy belter that made my ears ring and tensed muscles in my body that hadn't been activated since my last prostate exam, which is to say never.

Then Annika said two words that hit me like a knuckle in the solar plexus.

"It's Cameron," she said. She ran her fingers through her dark curls, then clenched a handful in each fist. "I mean it is and it isn't."

"How do you know it's Cameron at all? The body looks like it's caving in. The face..."

"It's written right here." She ran her finger along a metal plate riveted to the contraption that was embossed "Cameron Block, Specimen B." It even included the same in Braille, so the blind would catch on sooner than me.

I steadied myself against a stack of cubes and noticed a power cord that ran from the techno-tomb to the floor, along the crevice where the floor and wall met and then up the length of the far corner to an industrial ceiling lamp. It was jacked into the lamp with a wad of electrical tape. Before pot was legal-ish, growers would jerry rig hydroponics to grow weed in storage units in the much the same way. It never struck me as a place to stash a body.

"How can it be Cameron and not Cameron?" I said. "He have a secret evil twin?" After the words were out, it occurred to me that Cam would be the evil twin.

"Not a twin. It's Cameron. But not our Cameron."

"Clone?"

"Doppelgänger. From a parallel universe."

"How can you tell?"

Annika stepped up to the contraption. She turned the latches and the top popped up a quarter inch. She opened the lid. The stench made me gag. If shit could die, that's how it would smell. Annika, ever the scientist, was unfazed and proceeded to undo the corpse's pants. She peeked inside, raised an eyebrow and closed the lid.

"Yeah, no, that's not Cameron."

"How...?

Annika glowered back at me.

"Never mind," I said.

Annika stewed and bit the nail of her murderer's thumb. I had to ask.

"Did you do this?" I waggled my thumb at her – an accusatory gesture.

"If I were going to murder Cameron, I'd kill the right one."

"Then who did this?"

"Cameron, I suspect."

"You're saying Cameron killed... himself?"

"In a manner of speaking, yes."

"What do you even call that? 'Quantum suicide?'"

"No. That's something else."

"'Quantum suicide' is already a 'thing?' I can't keep up with you people," I said.

Annika helped me put the lid back on the box. Then something caught her eye. It was another row of boxes cannily camouflaged as one though a bit smaller than the last. "There's another one," she said. "Oh, no."

"Who do you think is in it?" I asked, but Annika was ahead of me. What little color there was in her face blanched away in an instant, leaving her lips a pale blue. "Help me," she said as she rushed to the lid and started prying it away. I was there in a flash and together we wrestled the lid open and let it drop to the floor. Inside was another sarcophagus.

"You don't think it's…"

Her steely eyes shot through me and I knew I was to perish the thought.

"I mean, Cam would kill himself but he wouldn't kill a kid, would he?" I reasoned aloud. But Annika couldn't hear me, she just kept chanting "No, no, no," to herself as she wiped the condensation from the portal to see the face inside. "Oh, no," she repeated. Then she pressed her thumb against the embossed metal plate with the occupant's name.

"Is it…?"

Annika sighed, her head bowed. I moved toward her, my hands suddenly on the lean biceps inside her sleeves. She shook her head and motioned to the nameplate.

"Alexandria Ashe, Specimen B."

We shared a silent moment, mutually relieved that it wasn't Jude. I heard a rhythmic thudding and scanned the confines of the storage locker for what was making it.

"It's your heart," said Annika. I plopped down onto a box and took deep breaths until all my systems were no longer cranked to eleven.

"Give me the phone," I said.

"Why?"

"I'm acquainted with a detective," I said as I cued up the text app.

"What are you doing?"

"I've got a friend on the force. I'm going to let her know what –"

"We don't have time," Annika interrupted.

"No time for a text?" I said. I texted the address to Detective Shane anyway.

Annika and I locked up the unit and wound our way back through the corridors. I stopped at the counter on the way out.

"Heads up," I said to the guy at the counter. "The cops will be here in a few minutes if you've got anything to flush."

His cratered face twisted as if to say, "Whatever." But a beat outside the door, I turned to see him scramble to the men's room.

Fresh from the windowless storage building, the skies seemed brighter than before – but then they always did in Lumaville, where the golden apples of the sun are natural, organic and wax.

Then it came to me:

"Rip Van Winkle," I said. "That what RVW stands for."

Annika clucked her tongue and slowly nodded. She knew I was right.

26.
Come up to the Lab

Annika dashed through the university quad – I tried to keep pace. We passed the Dick sculpture and toward the balustrade of the Pataphysics Department. Annika flung the door wide and Alfred Jarry kept his bronzed eye on us as we huffed up the stairs to the second-story lab. Annika's fingers danced on the security keypad but it didn't unlock. She entered the key code sequence again. Again, nada.

Annika rested her head against the FMRL door sign and closed her eyes. She was thinking – deeply – the same way she would sometimes at home and in college and in the all-girls high school where they assumed she was mentally ill and made her see a counselor, whom she seduced into recommending her for early graduation with little more than unbuttoning the top of her uniform.

Cameron had changed the door code to the lab but she knew there had to be a workaround. For kicks, I tried the code that worked at the storage unit but the beeping annoyed Annika and it didn't work anyway.

"Duh," she said. "I had it backwards. My mind has been doing that lately."

"It's all the designer drugs we did in the 90s," I joked but she actually seemed to agree.

The door opened.

Inside the lab was dark – closed for the day. After hours. It was like strolling into a toy shop at night. If there were dolls, they were winking and the toy soldiers were training their miniature rifles on us. It looked like the power had been cut or like some fatal electromagnetic pulse had silenced all the gadgets and finally proved Cameron's digital mortality.

Annika dropped her ass on the cube-shaped ottoman to catch her breath or light a smoke. She rummaged her pockets, found a broken cigarette and set to repairing it.

"Where's the coffee bot?" I asked.

"You don't need coffee, it'll just elevate your anxiety."

"My anxiety?" I said. "You know something I don't?"

She looked at me as if to say "volumes." Instead, she said, "While you were playing art critic at that gallery, I arranged a deal. With Cameron."

"I know, but why does it sound so ominous now?"

"Because it was a deal with Cameron so it's inherently a bad deal," she said. "Our boy is okay. He's been put to work bug-testing 'The Knights of Skeldaria 2.0.'"

"He'll be pissed that we brought him back," I said.

"No. He needs to go home," she said. "This hasn't been a vacation for him."

"Did you talk to him?"

"Yes," she said but didn't elaborate. "The less you know, the better."

"Is he meeting us here?"

"No," she said. "Gotta go there."

"Then why are we at the lab?"

"Because that's how you get there."

She rolled the repaired cigarette onto her lip and clicked her lighter seven times before the flame came to life and briefly lit the room. Annika's own shadow loomed over her shoulders like a bird of prey.

"You're sure Jude is okay?"

She chinned up and nodded as she exhaled a thin stream of smoke toward a window that was closed.

"Oh, shit," she said. "Smoke detectors." She pointed to the cushion next to me – my cue to use it to fan away the smoke as she opened a window. Beneath the cushion I found a plastic green medallion. Printed on it were the words, "I'm Ok." Jude nicked it from old Mac's door. I decided this was a sign from the universe. Then I decided it was sign from Jude. Then I decided it was just a sign from Mac's door that anyone visiting the home might have lifted as a trophy. This chilled me until I realized that no one visiting harm upon Mac would link themselves to the scene with a memento mori. And this is why I should have been an investigative reporter rather than hacking A and E stories, I thought. Yes, it was a sign from Jude, who, if I was decoding Annika's fidgets and laconic directives correctly, was no longer in this universe.

Annika darted back to me as I slipped the medallion into my pocket.

"Let's go," she said as she dragged me by my wrist into Cameron's office.

"This is where he does it," she said. Stood to reason, I thought. Really, who doesn't do something illicit in the office? Except it's usually corporate malfeasance or blowjobs – not bending time and space to one's odd ambition.

The office was decorated like a Gen X male fantasia. A road sign, "Slow Children at Play," was hung lazily on the wall next to some tony microbrew advert. A signed 8x10 of Carrie Fisher in her Princess Leia slave garb hung cockeyed on the wall above an unopened blue Snaggletooth action figure from the Sears Roebuck *Star Wars* cantina set. Imported picture discs of seminal 80s bands from the UK were suspended by fish line in a constellation around a replica red telephone box. I remembered that the evil kids were always anglophiles.

To the untrained eye, Cameron's digs probably looked like a case of arrested development. But this wasn't merely the man-cave of a mid-40s dude having a nostalgia fest. The pedigree of the collection and the precision with which it was curated was meant to distract from the man behind the curtain. Cameron was the fucking wizard.

Annika pressed the phone into my hand.

"It's ready," she said. She glanced at her watch. "This is the window of opportunity."

"And that's the door, the door of walking away from this sci-fi bullshit until I know where I'm going," I said. "Let me rephrase that – I'm not going end up like your piano, am I?"

Annika put her face close to mine, not for a kiss but for a whisper. She wasn't trying hide her words, we were alone after all. She was trying to soften the blow. She knew what she was about to say would break a better man. What she didn't count on was what I lacked in fortitude I made up in irony. I made Sisyphus look like a pinchaser down at LumaLanes. It's not that I could take it – I couldn't – but I could file it, somewhere deep within me, behind the seventy sheets of Gregg Ruled reporter's notebook that weighed in my breast pocket and kept my heart that crucial degree above frozen. Plus, all the booze and pills had done the job on my short-term memory I wished they'd done on my long-term. If I didn't instantly forget what Annika said to me, I could at least tragically ignore what was foretold.

Except this time.

She whispered.

"Really. Are you sure?" I asked.

She nodded.

Sonofabitch. Still, you had to admire the sinister touch.

Annika caressed my face with her white knuckle. She pressed her weird thumb against my chin.

"Are you sure?" she said. "It might be suicide, you know."

"That's why I'm going solo."

"Don't be a hero, Fergus. It doesn't work on you."

Somehow, with Annika, I was always a supporting character in my own movie.

"Anyway, you have to stay here," I said. "Someone's got to be here when I send Jude back. If I'm not."

Annika considered this.

"I can't tell if your argument is appealing to my sense of logic or my sense of self-preservation," she said.

"What do I do?" I asked, looking at the glowing screen of the phone on which was some eight-bit graphic of a sword and skull. It was *The Knights of Skeldaria* app in action. "Should I step into the phone booth?"

"You're not Superman," she said. It was a *Doctor Who* reference, but whatever. "The app is cued. You just have to tap the screen."

"That's it?"

"That's it," she said. "And be careful."

I let her words sink in and then I said the coolest line I've probably said in a decade.

"You can't go through the looking glass without getting scratched."

Annika kissed me hard.

"I love you," I said. And I might have meant it.

"I know," she said.

I took a deep breath and hovered my thumb over the app. Before I let it fall, all I could think about was how many times this woman has sent me sailing to Byzantium.

27.

Novus Alarum

I have it on good authority (well, Wikipedia) that it takes 3.7 seconds to fall 220 feet. This is precisely 3.7 seconds longer than it took to arrive over the rainbow.

There wasn't a vortex, no widening gyre, no waiting for the Polaroid to develop or dust to settle. The *2001* psychedelic light show was canceled, the *Vertigo*-zoom fell through – Buntel Eriksson's jump cuts seemed eternities by comparison. I blinked and, just as Jude had described his own woebegotten arrival, I was elsewhere. But where?

Annika's words came back to me with the salt wind that blew through my hair.

It was a balmy Fall day; late afternoon fog drifted over the span.

The waning sun started its dip into the Pacific but not without first painting its glow on the Golden Gate Bridge. International Orange – the color the steel was primed in order to prevent corrosion. It wasn't meant to be permanent but that's the thing about the bridge – what's done is done.

Commute traffic was gnarled mid-way on the Bay side. There was a commotion ahead that I couldn't see from my sidewalk vantage just past the toll plaza. But I had my suspicions, especially since the toll takers had yet to be replaced by the digital automata that replaced them.

I fact-checked with a goateed bro in a sports jersey.

"What's going on?" I asked as he dropped the camera from his face.

"Jumper," he deadpanned.

Yep. Annika was right. Cameron Block had invited me to *My Own Private Inferno*. Old, familiar songs burbled from the radios of cars that inched their way toward Marin County. A fog horn belched below the bridge and when it ended, a smarmy voice chortled, "Welcome back."

It came from a late-model convertible, some kind of extravagant electric coupe, more concept than car. The vehicle pulled alongside the curb, quietly pacing me, timed to my gait as if rehearsed. I didn't turn and kept walking as Cameron Block kept talking.

"Well, it's not really back,'" he continued. "But it's close enough for our purposes."

In the peripheral vision of my left eye I could see dour Jude in the passenger seat. He looked more bored than scared. In fact he didn't look scared at all – more like miffed.

On cue, Cameron cranked his car radio as an afternoon shock jock blared, "We gotta guy contorting the commute in both the northbound and southbound lanes on the Bridge as authorities try to talk him down. We've all been there people, we all know what's on his mind – with Mick Jones on lead vocals, from 'Combat Rock,' it's The Clash with 1981's 'Should I Stay or Should I Go?'"

The guitar was high and tight, the lyric throaty and plaintiff, "Darling you got to let me know, should I stay or should I go?"

I was no longer walking. A knot in my gut cinched hard and tight. I was vibrating, my blood was just shy of reaching a boil. I turned.

Cameron sat grinning, drumming his fingers on the

wheel, lip-synching the words. In the passenger seat, Jude glowered as if in after-school detention. Cameron stopped the car, which raised the ire of the driver behind him. He gestured to 'go around' with his middle finger.

"You okay?" I asked Jude above the din.

"Yeah," he hollered back from the car. "Been playing a shit-ton of 'The Knights of Skeldaria' so he could see how I cracked it."

Cameron shrugged and shouted. "I'm not above a little child labor, so sue me."

"And also, he's a dick," Jude volunteered, which earned a quick flick on the head from Cameron.

I sighed, looked at my boots. I never shined them as much as I should but I never noticed until now. Cameron turned down the tunes.

"Impressed yet?"

"Why here, man? Why does it have to be here?"

Cameron smiled. "It's always here," he said. "It's a tradition at this point."

"I have no idea what you're talking about."

"*You* don't, but a lot of losers just like you sure did," he said. "There are levels within levels at play, man. You're not a game designer, so you won't understand, but you have proven a very dependable variable in a very particular use-case scenario."

"The universe is a game and you've found a way to cheat," I said.

"*Universes* plural – and not 'cheat,'" Cameron said. "Win. You know how many times you fuck this up?" He snorted. "Every time. And it's beautiful because it puts so many wonderful outcomes in motion. You thought this was a big day for you? It's a big day – period. You – right here, right now – are an inflection point to a causality that makes it all possible. For me."

Flattered as I was to be so damn useful in a megalomaniac's master plan, I had my doubts about consistency. I mean, there still was free will after all and I was feeling pretty free and willful at the moment.

"It's always the same?" I said as I stepped to the car and took in an eyeful of the luxury interior. My eyes met Jude's as he hovered his hand over the buckle of his seatbelt.

"There's variations," Cameron said. "This little shit is a new wrinkle but he's proven valuable at debugging the game. Had more holes than I realized. There's probably little shits like this all over the multiverse at this point. But by and large the result is the same."

Jude clicked the seat belt as Cameron's hand came down heavy on his shoulder.

"Whoa there, partner," Cameron said. "I need the phone first."

"Don't give it to him," Jude said. "He's a psycho!"

Cameron's laugh came out like smoke rings – halting and self-conscious. Ha. Ha. Ha.

"You know what Einstein said about insanity, right? It's doing the same thing over and over and expecting different results," he quoted. "That makes me the sanest person I know because every time we do this, I get the exact same results and the rewards are, well..."

Then with a cluck, wink and two finger guns, he added, "You're perfect, Daedalus Howell, don't change a thing."

"So how do we do this?"

Business made Cameron serious.

"You give me the fucking phone and I send you and the Boy Wonder back."

I reached into my breast pocket and was immediately slapped across the gut with panic. Sure, the phone was there. And my own phone was in my own pocket. And, yes, I felt like one of those workaholic assholes with two mobiles. But that wasn't the problem. Or at least it wasn't Cameron's problem. For him, everything was right where it was supposed to be.

Cameron laid in.

"Ironic that you came to save one kid only to watch another one die."

Jude looked at me.

"What does he mean?"

"Don't play dumb, Jude, you know what he means."

I took my *own* phone out of my pocket, the one without the Willogen sticker and held it out, so that they could see it. Cameron straightened his back in the driver's seat.

"There we go, give me the McGuffin," he said and looked at his watch. "Come on, man. Aren't you on deadline? We don't have eternity."

Jude looked at the phone, then looked me dead in the eye and subtly nodded.

Cameron smiled his wolfish smile and arched a well-practiced eyebrow.

"But there's always infinity."

Minus one, asshole.

I threw my phone to Jude who leapt from his seat and caught it between his palms. In a beat, his foot was atop the doorlock and he sprung from the car and into my arms. I landed him on the sidewalk as he panted "Follow me!" before jetting down the pedestrian walkway and disappearing into the crowd of passersby.

"Mothefucker!" Cameron yelled and beat the wheel of the car. He tried to get out but it was a false start since he was still buckled in. I enjoyed the comedy for a millisecond and sprinted off after Jude. Over my shoulder I saw Cameron ditch the car and dart through the stationary traffic. Drivers behind his parked car honked to no avail. Apart from messing with the space-time continuum, Cameron

Block was messing with Marin County commuters, which, under any other circumstances, is admirable.

Tourists congested the bridge's pedestrian entrance. Dozens of impromptu fashion shoots bloomed with preening teens and travelers unaware of the human drama a few hundred feet away. They wore brightly colored windbreakers and fanny packs and I pushed through like a weed in a bouquet.

Just ahead, traffic was stopped on the northbound side. Police lights flashed. Two squad cars were parked in the far lane along the walkway. One cop was on his walkie talkie, the other was directing the growing crowd to keep a wide berth. Some brandished mobile phones like the reaper's own paparazzi, their camera phones high above their heads, wrists stretched naked from their sleeves.

In the middle of the mayhem was 1K, my erstwhile intern. Perched on the rail of the bridge he looked younger and small against the vista of the Bay Area skyline and the hungry sea below.

"You can't save him!" Cameron shouted at me from a few paces back. "It's not even him for crissakes!"

He was right. And he was catching up. I wended through elbows and purses and lollygaggers. There was a reason Jude led me this way, even if I couldn't save 1K. Perhaps it was to try.

I elbowed passed the onlookers getting as close as I could get. I hollered his name until our eyes met over a sea of police hats and comb-overs. A burly cop stopped me cold, body-blocking me such that his seven-point star caught on the placket of my shirt.

1K shifted a leg over the ledge and cried toward me, "What are you doing here?"

"You know him?" the officer said back to 1K in a calm, low voice.

"He's my editor," he said. "Let me talk to him!"

The cop looked me hard in the eye.

"You done this before?"

I nodded – rather than go into specifics. The cop turned his body like a door on a hinge and I stepped toward my intern. Or at least this rumpled, sad, version of him about to jump off the Golden Gate Bridge.

Cameron caught up but was stopped by the same cop. Jude, I could only assume, was hiding amongst the guts and boobs swaddled in San Francisco Giants sweatshirts and yoga clothes that were backfilling the perimeter of the spectacle.

"What the hell are you doing?" I asked. The cop who let me in cleared his throat and pinched the bridge of his nose.

1K took a deep breath and screwed up his face in an effort to dam up the tears.

"What do you think I'm doing? The 1K story," he said, straddling the rail. "I'm number one-thousand. This is my purpose. This is the only meaningful thing I can do. You should be happy – I'm giving you the end to your story."

"*My* story?" I said. "For fuck's sake, what about *your* story?"

"This *is* my story. I don't care anymore. I just don't care. I don't know why anyone cares."

His eyes were wet. He wiped them on the sleeve of his hoodie then squinted at me for longer than was polite but I let him continue until I couldn't take it.

"What?" I asked.

"You look like shit, man" he said. "I mean you really look like shit."

"Yeah, but I have a higher life expectancy than you. So, you know, fuck you."

The cop, not a fan of my technique, mock-coughed into his fist and shifted his weight from foot to foot.

1K stymied a laugh, then looked down toward the Bay then back at me. His eyes searched mine but he didn't know what he was looking for. I knew I had to work up something, so I stalled.

"I don't know what I'm supposed to say to you," I said.

"Really?" he said, incredulous. His cheeks were rosy with windburn. "You're supposed to say it gets better. So? Does it?"

I thought for a few seconds. I mean, I really applied the full complement of my mental resources to the problem, such as they were. I thought of my ruined life, the bad blood and broken hearts, the squandered potential and moments when I said too little or said too much and came up consistently on the wrong side of the ledger. I factored in that I'm not, by strictest definition, a normal person and figured if I was it would probably net out anyway.

"No," I said. "It might not get any better per se. But it sure as hell doesn't get any worse than this. Honestly... it just gets weirder. But it's all uphill from here. Like, I don't know, Sisyphus or something," I said and shrugged. "Okay, bad example. But..."

Under his breath, the cop muttered, "Shit, buddy, you're making *me* wanna jump."

I looked back at the crowd. The faces reflected back my own bewilderment. One guy had let an ice cream cone melt over his knuckles so transfixed was he by my flailing talk-down. Only one face shone back with encouragement: Jude's. His head bobbed amongst the cleavage of an apparent bachelorette party – one of the women wore a crown made of miniature dicks.

Cameron, relegated to the rear of the ensemble caught my eyeline, traced it to Jude, and started to make his way. Before I could make a plan, 1K cried out, "Why do we even fucking bother – with the newspaper, with the stories, with anything? It's all bullshit. And I'm tired of bullshit. I'm tired of being a loser and feeling like *this* all the time."

He shifted his grip. The sweat from his palms darkened the rust hue of the girder.

I looked back to see Cameron cross to Jude and stand behind him.

"Why do we fucking bother, man? Just tell me why we do any of it. The truth. It's all meaningless, isn't it? Just tell me."

"Hold on."

I didn't have the words yet. So, I went with action. I pressed my gut against the guardrail and swung my leg until the ankle of my boot hooked on the rail. Two tries. But once done I was able to slide my leg over to the knee and with some harrumphing get my ass on the rail. It wasn't elegant but with a couple heaves more and a tacit grip on the cable (they are thicker than they look), I was next to 1K.

Below, a freighter cut through the Bay so from my vantage it passed through my legs. On the other side, Cameron covered Jude's eyes with his hand and smiled. Had it not been satirical, the gesture was almost human.

The cops pressed the crowd a few feet further away. What, were they afraid of the splashback?

1K looked offended, like I stepped too close to him in the locker room. He gritted his teeth against his tears. I reached out my hand. My arm was unsteady against the gale. My coat and shirt billowed like ship sails.

"One reason!" 1K repeated. He took a hand off the rail to make a number one, which proved even more precarious in the wind. Then he upped the ante and hovered a foot over the blue doom 220 feet below. The crowd gasped. Through a veil of tears, he wailed, "Why?"

I set my jaw and looked over the galloping horses of the

sea. Then I remembered. And I told him. Slowly, patiently and per the Associated Press Stylebook:

"Because," I said sternly, "We're newspapermen."

The wind stopped for a moment. Everything still, quiet. Quiet enough for me to hear 1K whisper to himself, "We're newspapermen...?"

"It's not a compliment," I said. "But only a newspaperman would dangle himself off the side of a bridge for the sake of a stupid-ass story. And this, my friend, is a stupid ass story."

"I always thought so."

"But it's the story we're in now," I said. "Even in the bad stories, hope conspires. And that's the job, man – you find the thing we gotta believe in to get through. You got a bunch of horseshit and busted dreams? That's the goddamn recipe for redemption, man. Your life is meaningless and you're a shell of a person? Perfect – you're free to make meaning without self-interest. You think you're the only idiot to go down this path? Brother, everyone is on this path – but fortunately we got assholes like you to gin up enough column inches, enough pages, enough reasons to remind us that, sure, life is cheap – but it's worth it."

The young man looked at me dumbfounded. The crowd hushed. Jude pried Cam's fingers from his eyes.

1K dropped his head, shook it, slowly, reckoning with something heaving in his chest. His sad eyes were on me. He looked me over, looked quizzical and asked, "Dude, are you wearing a Superman shirt?"

I looked down at my action figure outfit. My shirt had lost its top buttons in the tussle to 1K. And, yes, beneath it was was my raggedy-ass, faded Superman shirt.

"That," he said, "That is the coolest thing ever."

It kind of was.

"You know why?" 1K said laughing. "Because Superman's true identity… He's a newspaperman too. What a fucking loser!"

I laughed. 1K laughed. Even the cop cracked a smile, but only for a moment.

"What's the next move?" asked 1K.

"We get down," I said. "The dry way."

He nodded and took the vital step homeward. The crowd applauded.

When I turned my boot to make the same step, the heel caught on the top of the rail and my good knee bent the bad way and the bad knee tried to make good but...

I slipped.

Like a bad dance, I couldn't get my footing straight and the wind wasn't helping. Gravity had begun her seduction – I was going to fall. For a moment, I'll admit, it didn't matter. A lonely impulse of delight drove to this tumult in the clouds and I could almost accept it. But small hands wrung themselves into the tail of my coat and pulled me back to earth.

I folded onto the pedestrian walkway. It was a hard landing but at least it wasn't far. 1K helped me to my feet. I expected it was Jude who pulled me back from the abyss. Instead, standing in front of me was a very old man, dapper and topped in a straw hat.

"Almost took a powder there, Clark Kent," he said. He brushed me off and patted me on the shoulder. "We newspapermen gotta look out for each other," he winked. He didn't know me but I knew him somewhere else as Mac.

The crowd parted for me and 1K.

"Stand back, people," bellowed the cop.

I looked for Jude and couldn't see him. But I saw Cameron trotting through northbound traffic toward Vista Point.

1K put his arm around my shoulder.

"Fergus. Thank you," he said. "I owe you, man."

I shook my head.

"We're even," I said. "I mean, you need lot of help and you better get it. But you and me? We're even."

"Roger that," he said. "So, now what?"

I started after Cameron, heading north on the pedestrian walkway.

"Let's go!

28.
In the Key of Block

At 1.7 miles, the Golden Gate Bridge was once the longest suspension bridge in the world. I didn't know which bridge bested it and took the title, but I did know that Jude would have traversed as quickly. He was a contender for a five-minute mile and was very nearly at Vista Point, the tourist stop on the bridge's north side, when 1K and I started after him. Cameron Block was close behind him until blundering into a group photo that clogged the pathway and lost him his pace.

1K and I continued like salmon swimming upstream until 1K suddenly stopped cold and turned on his heels. His eyes were on a man into whom we nearly collided, whose nose was inches from his phone. The man kept on, however, blithe, blissful and clearly in his own universe – literally.

Kit Fergus, five years younger, taller than I realized and blessedly ignorant of the massive glitch in the Matrix I'd brought with me, was on his way to get the story I just killed. He didn't notice us, concerned as he was with his looming big break, the tousle-haired woman in his bed, the Mini Cooper he financed on pure ambition.

1K stared at me, suspicious, as he leaned against the

guardrail and chewed at his lower lip as if to say "WTF, man?"

To him, I was a spare piece in what he heretofore assumed was the completed puzzle.

He looked toward Kit's back and took a deep breath, ready to shout, surely, but relented when I gestured to shhh.

"Okay, so – who *are* you? Who are you, *really*?" 1K asked. "Because *that* was my editor."

"Trust me, I know," I said.

"Then who are *you*?" he asked again. His tone was a mix of awe and accusation, as if I was both an angel and an identity thief.

I took a moment to square it with myself. I wasn't Kit Fergus, that was for sure. The schmuck walking toward San Francisco and the defining moment that would never happen – that was Kit Fergus. I'd gone too far down the road to ever be him again. And after all was said and done, that was fine with me.

"I'm Daedalus Howell," I said.

"You're what?"

I said it again. Something lit in 1K's eyes.

"But…"

"I know. It's weird," I said. "Seeing him, seeing me. Don't think too hard on it. We live in strange times."

"No, I mean, isn't that name from a Buntel Eriksson film?" he said, incredulous.

Why is it young people always ruin all the cool obscure shit?

"Yeah. It's from a Buntel Eriksson film. The good one," I said. "Relatively speaking."

"Don't you want to talk to him?" 1K asked, pointing to the black coat disappearing into the crowd ahead.

"He wouldn't listen anyway," I said. "But if you want to score a byline, spec seven hundred words on why Rifka

Benco shot first in 'The Plastic Spy.' If I remember correctly, there's a 20-inch newshole in the B section. Your editor will take it."

1K nodded vigorously, then got ahold of himself and saluted me before drifting into the tide of tourists, until I could no longer see him, just as I could no longer see his editor. Not even in a mirror.

When I reached Vista Point, Jude was nowhere to be seen. Cameron had his eyes in a pair of coin-op binoculars, which he swiveled to survey the parking lot. This made it easy for him to spot me as I wheezed into the parking lot.

"You're developing some serious crow's feet, my man," he jeered from twenty feet away. "You should use more sunscreen."

He stepped out from behind the binocular stand and did a little dance.

"This is where it gets interesting," he said.

I wouldn't have bothered trying to divine the meaning of Cameron's cryptic words had I not spied the pristine, new red-and-white Mini Cooper parked near the flagpole at Vista Point's visitor center entrance. Just as Kit Fergus had parked it. Just as I had parked it – or one quite like it – in another time, another place. The flagpole cast a long, late afternoon shadow across the hood, as did the small figure hiding in front of it.

"Hey, Jude. Don't let me down," Cameron sang. He started improvising, "Take a sadsack and make him better..."

Cameron gave up on the lyrics and hummed the melody instead as he reached into his pocket and pulled out a small jumble of mechanical mayhem, which he proceeded to methodically unfold. It looked like set of brass knuckles humping a Swiss army knife – apart from the barrel and trigger.

"Apache Knuckle Duster," he said. "Nineteenth century.

French. Rare, collectable and completely unrecognizable as anything beyond a novelty."

"Why do they call it 'Apache' if it's French?" I said.

"Why do they call French fries French fries?" he replied. "Who fucking cares? That's the problem with people like you, man. You sweat the minutiae. The small moments. Think of the technology that got us here. We could go anywhere. The Renaissance, or the birth of Christ. But most people? People like you – they would just go back to moments in their own lives. And not even the best moments. They would go to the moments – nay, the moment – where they fucked up. The one that got away, the job they should've taken – because the intellect of man is forced to choose," said Cameron. "They way I do it, however, it's not just a second chance – it's an infinite amount of chances. Big plans afoot. We were just beginning. And I had it wired, man. Perfected it. Except for one variable. One time. This time."

"And what was that?" I asked.

"You."

Cameron turned the barrel of the gun such that he could peer down a chamber. He fished a bullet from his shirt pocket and pushed it in with his thumb and gave the barrel a spin.

"There. All full," he said, then he announced to anyone within ear shot, "Jude! If you don't come out, I'll shoot him. You know I will."

Cameron pointed the gun at me. As he had anticipated, no one gave a shit.

"Come on, Jude," he continued, "Don't be a punk."

"Be a punk," I yelled back.

Silence and seagulls. After a beat: "He'll shoot you," Jude's small voice quavered from behind the Mini. "He did it before."

Cameron looked satisfied. He moved swiftly to the car.

"I knew I could leverage you guys against each other," he said as he pulled Jude up by the collar.

Cameron used the gun to motion me to the car. I went.

"Look at you two assholes," he said and shook his head. "Give me the phone, kid."

Jude looked at me with wet eyes. I nodded and he produced the phone.

"I'm sorry," Jude said to me.

"Don't be sorry, Jude," I said. "Cameron's the sorry one."

Jude looked at me, then stared Cameron dead in the eye.

"He killed my parents," he said. "I think."

Cameron laughed. "That's rich, kid, because in another universe, you're their abortion".

"What's he talking about?" I said to Jude but Cameron answered.

"You have no idea how fucked the timeline gets in some places," he said. "And frankly, it's usually your fault. I've been cleaning your messes for decades. I can't tell if it's karma or kismet at this point. But nobody gets in my way."

"I know. You even killed yourself. I found your handy work in the storage unit."

Cameron laughed.

"Yeah, that," he sighed. "I guess I'm one of the few people who can say I killed myself and lived to talk about it."

"You're a murderer," I said.

"Technically, that was more like 'quantum suicide,'" he said. "I kept getting in my own way. It was irksome."

"And Ashe?"

"There was no way in hell I was going to let that bitch get her evil mits on this – again," he said. "I've had to clean a lot of shit up, Howell. I'm actually one of the good guys."

"Then why Mac?"

"Who?" he said, but we were both distracted by the

music suddenly emanating from his body. First, none of us recognized it but then it clicked – the Imperial March from *Star Wars*. It was a ringtone. Cameron used his free hand to fish the phone out of his pocket.

"There's reception out here?" He looked at the phone. I watched Cameron do the mental math.

"You sonofabitch, this is your phone!"

Cameron threw the phone at me. I caught it. The caller ID said it was Adriane, the Editrix.

"It's my editor. I have to take it."

"Daedalus Howell," I said, doing my thing.

Cameron glowered at me, dumbfounded.

"Where the fuck is my story, Howell?" Adriane brayed into the phone. "You told me some fantastic tale, so where the fuck is it, man?"

"Listen, I'm on it, it's just that I'm in the middle of something – "

"Get off the fucking phone so I can shoot you!" Cameron shouted.

"Don't get shot," Adriane's voice crackled through the phone. "Until you file the story."

She hung up as Cameron spat on the ground.

"Okay, very clever, Mr. Howell," he said as he kept the Apache Knuckle Duster trained in one hand and patted me down with the other.

"For crissakes, just give it up," he said.

"But I'm enjoying the shiatsu," I said, so he started pelting me with the gun.

"How's that?"

"Stop! Don't hurt him," Jude yelled.

"Inside left pocket," I said. "Next to the reporter's notebook."

With a flurry of tugs and tosses like he was disarming some film noir gunsel, Cameron finally found the phone,

Willogen sticker and all. His wolf grin brightened the shadow that peppered his face.

"And the key to the Mini."

"Fuck you," I said. "It's not even the same car, Cameron."

"Seriously, the key. Now!" he commanded as the poked the small knife blade of the weapon into the gristle of my shoulder.

"You gypsy dildo bastard!" I grimaced. It stung like hot ice. "That's my new coat," I said through gritted teeth. I tossed Cameron the key. He caught it and clicked the remote button. Sure as shit, the Mini's amber parking lights flashed and its door locks stood at attention.

Cameron looked at me and Jude and snickered.

"Now what're you gonna do?" he rhetorically taunted. "Write a book about it?"

"I might," I said. Perhaps a tad defensively.

"Well, your ending sucks," he said.

He got into the Mini and buckled up. After a beat, the window rolled down. He reached his hand out, clutching the phone.

"This was your ticket to greatness," he said. "You had the whole world – no – you had the whole multiverse in your hand and you didn't even know it. Typical of guys like you. That goes for you too, Jude, you little shit."

Jude gave him the finger as Cameron swiped his thumb over the phone's face.

A very loud whoosh cleaved the sky.

Cameron looked up. Jude looked up.

I looked up. I squinted into the late afternoon sun and could just make out the silhouette of something careening toward earth – what? A bird, a plane? My visual cortex processed it within nanoseconds but my mind rejected the results as quickly. Ditto my auditory cortex, which was suddenly tasked with interpreting the roaring clang of 88 keys – 52 white and 36 black – played simultaneously on a piano. Or more precisely, Annika's piano – and not "played" so much as smashed into a heap of splintered wood and ivory and what was once a brand-new red-and-white Mini Cooper. And a man named Cameron Block.

"Holy fucking shit!" Jude shouted.

A woman screamed in the distance. I could hear the footsteps of the crowd beginning to trot up to the seen.

"What was that?" Jude asked.

"A piano," I said. "We were wondering where it went."

Oil and blood mixed into an obscene cocktail and puddled around the heap.

Cameron's outstretched arm projected from the wreckage like a swizzle stick from a tumbler. Albeit a shattered tumbler. I pried his fingers from their death grip and extracted the phone. It suffered little more than a Y-shaped crack in the screen. With some slushy groping I also fished free the key to the Mini.

It was time to go.

"Let's get the hell out of here," I said to Jude.

He nodded and wrapped his arms around me. He probably wouldn't say so but I knew it was a hug. I hit the app.

29.
On Deadline

Annika bolted up from Cameron's desk chair. She snubbed a cigarette out – the last of several question mark shaped butts lined on his desk – and rushed over to us. She ignored me completely and went straight for the boy. She hugged him hungrily, dug her fingers through his curls, begged him to tell her he was fine. He was and he held onto her just as tightly.

"What took you so long, damn it?"

"Oh, little things like getting a hole poked in me, that sort of shit," I said. "Also, we found your piano."

Annika didn't want to know. She just wanted to get on with the plan.

"Phone please."

I slapped it in her palm and she thumbed through the apps, readying Jude's return trip.

"We have to get him out of here before Cameron comes back."

Jude couldn't refrain a wicked smile.

"He's not coming back," he said.

Annika looked at me and my raised eyebrows confirmed it. She looked mildly impressed.

"Okay, kiddo," she said to Jude. "You ready?"

But Jude's attention was already elsewhere. He was rapt by the reflection of the three of us in the glass wall of Cameron's office.

Annika took in the family portrait. Somewhere, sometime, it almost made sense.

"I can't let him go alone," she said under her breath. "I'm going with him."

"You're what?"

"I'm going with him," she said. She clasped a hand to the back of my neck to huddle. "He doesn't have anyone over there."

"I gathered that."

"And for crissakes, he found us," she said, then repeated "us" to emphasize it meant more than merely the objective case of "we."

"What should I do?"

"Someone has to stay here and make sure none of this can happen again."

"And I'm qualified, how?"

"Because you don't understand it," she said flatly. "So, you can't abuse it."

"Finally, my ignorance is an asset."

She brightened.

"It's more than that. You're you," she said. It sounded meaningful but I'm pretty sure it wasn't. "But, you have to understand – this is only the beginning. There's something very scary happening. Get some good people on your side, get some friends, assemble the Avengers – be prepared. Because the shit is coming down. Do you understand?"

She looked over my shoulder.

"Oh, no," she said and swallowed hard.

"The shit's already coming down isn't it?"

JCN had seen better days, but his prime directive was intact. So was his gun – another online antique, hastily wired where his robot hand had once been.

Instinctively, I enfolded Jude and Annika into my coat and became a human umbrella.

The shots came, rapid and rhythmic – thunk, thunk, thunk – like successive beats on a floor tom. The glass wall shattered and rained to the floor with the tinny timbre of a gamelan.

I didn't feel a thing.

JCN crumpled to the floor in a smoking heap of servos and blue spaghetti wire.

Heels crunched over the glass. I turned and was relieved to see Detective Shane stepping into the office as she let the spent clip fall to the floor.

"Got your text," she said to me, nonchalant. "Found your car. Also, you got a parking ticket."

"Goddamn it, Annika," I said. She had parked the car. Her eyes were on JCN.

"I hated that fucking robot."

"You're welcome," said Detective Shane.

"Thank you," Annika said, then turned to me, her face a shade paler. "We have to go. The quantum deadline."

"Just wait," said Shane. She pointed at Jude. "He belong to you?"

"Yes."

"Good," said Shane, slipping her Glock back into her shoulder holster. "Case closed."

I knelt to Jude and straightened his collar. I pressed my forehead to his.

"Listen, you deserve better than us and we know it," I said. "But we're rooting for you."

"I know," he said. "I'm rooting for you too."

"You know how to find me."

"You can find me too," he said, then tapped my forehead. "You're still Bizzaro."

"You're still Bizzaro's sidekick."

Annika put her hand on Jude's shoulder.

"It's time."

I nodded, stood up. Deep breath.

"You have a hole in your coat," Annika said softly.

"Don't – ouch! – stick your finger in it," I said but she already had.

"Gross." She wiped the blood from her finger onto my lapel – then went in for a big kiss. Everything vital in me vanished into her as she pulled me by my sideburns and locked her smoky lips onto mine. I would've passed out had Jude not cleared his throat from embarrassment.

Annika pushed me away.

"Don't say anything."

"I wasn't going to."

She smiled and hovered her thumb over the phone.

"Annie…" I said but in a blink, they were both gone.

Shane and I stood looking at each other for a very long and quiet moment.

"You smoke?" she asked, eyes on the desk.

"Not really."

"Me neither," she said and nodded.

I tossed her Annika's pack of cigarettes. She took two out and put each to her lip and lit them.

We sat on the couch in Cameron's office and smoked.

"They got a coffee machine here?"

"They do. But it's a robot," I said. "You'd just end up shooting it."

"Probably," she said.

I gestured to the spot where Annika and Jude had been and suddenly weren't.

"I'm sure you have questions."

"Forget it, Dade. It's Lumaville," she said. Shane blew a trio of smoke rings. "There's weirder shit than this going, man. This is only the beginning.

I believed her.

30.
Next

I tugged the ticket from the Mini's wiper and crumpled it into my pocket. Inside, I strapped in, adjusted the mirror and turned the key. She turned over and I rolled toward town.

Who will go drive with Fergus now?

At the pad, my apartment was still a mess. No transdimensional cleaning fairies had visited while I was out.

Before I could consider next steps (like moving to a hotel), my phone rang. No caller ID – probably my Editrix stalking me for the story. She was clever like that, blocking her ID. It wasn't my style to be late but I had to admit that I was savoring the sensation of being on deadline. Which is to say, I felt normal.

"Daedalus Howell…" I answered.

There was a long pause. Too long. I was about hang up until…

"I like the new jacket. Nice silhouette. Shame about the hole."

"Who is this?"

"I'm you're biggest fan." The voice wasn't a man, wasn't a woman – it was electronically filtered to some odd castrati

242

mid-point. It was using the same effect I'd heard when on the phone at Mac's place.

"You know what they never mention in your obituary, Howell?"

I parted the blinds of my window – nothing on the street.

"What they never mention is how, mythologically speaking, Daedalus built his own wings."

"I don't follow," I said as I trod the debris in my pad to look out the kitchen window.

"In the Labyrinth. Daedalus made wings of wax and feathers so he could fly like an angel."

"So what?" I said as I looked downstairs to the cafe below. I watched a young fellow on a mobile phone for a moment but then he put it back down on the table.

"In my book, that makes him a false angel," said the caller. "And that's even worse than a fallen angel."

I turned from the window, took a step and almost lost my footing as my boot slid on something slickening the tile.

Dark, viscous fluid pooled beneath the refrigerator door. The heel of my boot cut a clean slash through the coagulated puddle, above which small flies, barely perceptible amid the dust dancing in the afternoon light, darted and dove.

"What's in the fridge?" I said slowly into the phone. My breath was shallow and staccato. It was difficult to disguise the fear welling in my chest.

"Why don't you open it and see," said the caller.

My fingers trembled as I reached for the refrigerator door handle. I counted to three in my mind and gave it a yank.

I didn't realize how loud or long I screamed but it pleased the caller to no end.

"Never heard a Daedalus *howl* before," the caller snickered.

I leaned back against the sink and slid to the floor of

the narrow galley kitchen. Maggots writhed in and out of the ears but its black, open eyes were more horrifying – its gaze blank and pitiless as the sun. Space was cleared to fit the horns between the old takeout boxes on one side and the beer bottles on the other. A thick ring hung between its broad nostrils.

"I considered leaving it in your bed 'Godfather' style, but didn't know when you were coming home and wanted it to be fresh."

"Why a bull?" I asked between sharp breaths.

"You should know that, Daedalus," the caller said, hitting the syllables of my name as if each successive beat of the tongue was more disgusting than the last.

"Minotaur – right?"

"Yes," the caller hissed.

"Little meta, don't you think?"

"Yes," the caller hissed again. "I like that."

"Like what?" I spat back.

"Metataur."

"Oh, for crissakes," I sighed into the phone but the call ended.

I reached into the fridge and grabbed one of the beers next to the rotting head. I capped the bottle on the counter edge and took a tug. I stared at the bull, it stared at me, and I toasted the rough beast, its hour come round at last, slouching toward Lumaville…

The End

About the Author

Daedalus Howell began his media career as a paperboy in Petaluma, California, delivering the very newspaper that would hire him as a writer in his early 20s. Since then, he has written for the *San Francisco Chronicle, North Bay Bohemian, Sonoma Index-Tribune, Men's Health* and beyond. He lives and works in the San Francisco Bay Area.

Get on the list!

Sign up now to receive updates on Daedalus Howell's *Lumaville Labyrinth* series as well as news about appearances and special events. Visit DaedalusHowell.com/newsletter.

National Suicide Prevention Lifeline

1 (800) 273-8255
suicidepreventionlifeline.org

Lightning Source UK Ltd.
Milton Keynes UK
UKHW011428101022
410236UK00007B/1051